Mich

MW00977502

The Christmas
of Miracles

Four Sonkist Angels
Christian Publishing Company
Suwanee, GA
www.FourSonkistAngels.com
770-888-5515

The Christmas of Miracles
Copyright © 2005 Four Sonkist Angels
Christian Publishing Company
First Printing 2005

Library of Congress Control Number: 2004092252

Published by:
Four Sonkist Angels
Christian Publishing Company
www.FourSonkistAngels.com
info@FourSonkistAngels.com
Michelle@FourSonkistAngels.com
770-888-5515

ISBN: 0-9753117-0-0

Cover Design by Team Lensflair – Rio Meek, Jason Walton
Model for Cover – Katie Webster
Logo by PK Designs – Paul Inbody
Printing Company, United Graphics, Inc. – Kim Shaffer
Book Design and Typesetting by Just Your Type DTP, justyourtypedtp@earthlink.net

Printed in the United States by United Graphics Incorporated
2916 Marshall Ave, PO Box 559
Mattoon, IL 61938-0559
217-235-7161

✧

Dedication

For Joey, Frankie, Bailey and Katie

Dream big,
Believe in yourself,
Pray for guidance,
Seek counsel,
Read Proverbs,
Then...

you will be able to make wise decisions.

✧ ✧ ✧ ✧

Proverbs 13:20

"He who walks with the wise grows wise,
but a companion of fools suffers harm."

✧

Acknowledgements

Above all else, I need to thank God for guiding me through this book. The number of people he has placed in my path to make this book possible is unbelievable! This book would never have made it into your hands if it weren't for the following people.

Jim, my wise, realistic, loving husband – you are the perfect balance for me. I love you with every ounce of my being. You have been incredibly patient during the weekend and late night rewrites. You are such a wonderful father and husband. Your opinions were invaluable during the many decisions involved in publishing this book. Thank you for letting me be an optimistic dreamer and for becoming my greatest supporter. I love you forever, baby.

Joey, Frankie, Bailey and Katie – you have been my biggest encouragers during the writing of this book! You helped me all along with your opinions on everything from the cover of the book, to the ending. You have been incredibly patient when my thoughts and fingers were attached to the keyboard. I'm so proud of each of you. No matter what happens in life – you'll always have your faith and your family. I love you so very much.

Cathy Lee Phillips, my wonderful, diligent editor and teacher – I'm still in awe over the circumstances that brought us together. I have learned SO much working with you. You made me believe that my dreams could become reality. You didn't let me settle for mediocre when I was ready to be done. You KMITB when I needed it. Chili's, KAZzing, finding our Silver in the Slop and of course our Lord and Savior, Jesus Christ. You rock, girlfriend!

Matthew Hilger, my brilliant business director – Spalding Drive, kids number, UGA, Brumby dorm window, helping me study, party dawg. From Fortune 500 businessman to professional poker player, author and speaker – you're amazing! Internet Texas Hold'em paved the way for this book to be published. Thank you for teaching me the ropes in the publishing business.

Mom and Dad – You guys are the best parents in the entire world. Thank you so much for always encouraging me to write – even before I knew I wanted to be a writer. You always believed in me, no matter what I wanted to do. You taught me to believe in myself. You advise me when I need it and step back when I need space. You've always made me believe that you are proud of me no matter what I do, and you gave me my faith, that has given me stability in times when nothing else felt stable. I love you so much.

Nana and Baba Goose – You guys are awesome. I think I could have written a bomb and you guys would have loved it. I've never known anyone who has such unconditional pride and love for their family members. Baba – you seem hardcore, but you're really a teddy bear at heart. Nana, you passed my book along to everyone you knew – thank you so much for showing that kind of faith in me. Baba, I can't believe you read the book twice! I didn't even know you read books! Thank you. I love you both so much.

Dave and Eileen – I couldn't have asked for better inlaws. You guys are the best. Thank you so much for all the years you encouraged me to write a book. You planted a seed and made me wonder if it might be possible. You weren't even blood but you told me you thought I had talent. Your words of encouragement prodded me to finally pursue a longheld dream for me. Thank you.

My wonderful sister and friend, Shari – Thank you for your support and encouragement throughout this process. Thank you for your last minute proofreading. It was worth the wait. Lakehouse – New Years Eve – Cathy – that was totally a God thing. I love you.

Aunt Mimi – Thank you for using your "artist's eye" to help me tweak the book cover until it was just perfect. As I do not have the ability to visualize artistic things, your input was invaluable. You went through the entire book cover with me and gave me incredibly prompt advice. Thank you for encouraging me to get this book published too.

Lauren – Girlfriend – what would I have done without your proofreading? I'd have about 3000 more exclamation points, I'd still be switching up shook and nod, and my dates would be off if you hadn't encouraged me to double check the timing of events. Thank you for providing such excellent work for an incredibly reasonable price – free.

Lori and Stephanie – You both are such sweethearts. Lori, you are such an incredibly giving person. Thank you for all you've done for me and my family over the years. You just might be the nicest person I've ever met. Stephanie, you were the first person who read *The Christmas of Miracles* when I gave it out last Christmas. I couldn't have been more deeply moved than when you called me, crying, and said, "Your book is so touching! It is the best book I've ever read!" Thank you so much. Your words of encouragement still mean the world to me.

Terry – Thank you for your encouragement and willingness to proof several different rewrites. What an honor it was that you gave away your original copy of my book to a stranger you met at a research study. Thank you for your wonderful friendship. I love you.

Margot – Thank you for always offering me your honest opinion, and letting me know that I should take it with a grain of salt. I love that during my "voice rest" you could still hear me. I live for the summers and holidays when we can "talk" more frequently. What a wonderful friend you are. I love you.

Miriam – You are my true inspiration of finding God's blessing in difficult circumstances. Your peace and unwavering faith are beyond my comprehension. You are so right though – if you allow Him to, God can bring good out of the worst situations. I'm so thankful for you and our friendship. I love you.

Christine – You are incredibly gifted with patience and the art of listening. Thank you for sharing with me the ups and downs that went along with writing and publishing a book. Keep pushing me to workout, girl! I love you.

Dawn – Thank you for building me up and encouraging me in anything I ever want to pursue. I can't believe you married one of my husband's best friends! Is that cool or what? I miss our girls' night out. Seven kids between us? Who says we're busy?

Ann – thank you for always loving my precocious Katie. I would be at my wits end and bring her to you so I could get some writing done – and everytime I picked her up, you said, "She was an angel, as always." Thank you for brainwashing me… and Katie… into believing that. You are the best sitter anyone could ask for.

Mary, Lauren, Christine and Karen, my Northpoint small group buddies – thank ya'll for your prayers, your support and your love. I don't ever want to break apart from you guys. Ya'll are the best.

Carol, Jean and Kathy – my wonderful sis-in-laws and friends. I'm so blessed to have you guys. I love ya'll.

Creekside Wings – thank you for all your prayers that my writing and this book glorify God. I miss ya'll.

Jackie, Liz, Allison, Dr. Featherstone and Jan, Andy and Sandra Stanley, Scott Hearn, Richard Paul Evans, Nicholas Sparks and Clay Aiken – you all have touched my life in many different ways – some spiritually, some physically, some emotionally – some of you don't even realize it. Thank you.

Rio Meek at Lensflair Designs – You have been fabulous to work with. Thank you for your frequent and detailed communication. You have exceptionally high standards with regard to making sure the product is precisely what your customer is looking for. I am in awe at the hard work and dedication you devoted to making my book cover as incredible as I imagined it could be. I love it.

Ken Rada Photography – Ken, thank you for staying at Jones Bridge for as long as it took to get the perfect picture of my family for the back book cover. I love the way you do business and am thrilled to have so many great shots of my family – together and as individuals. Great job.

Sue of Just Your Type Desktop Publishing – You were great at teaching me the ropes in how to prepare a manuscript for the typesetter. Thank you for your patience in explaining things to me and in waiting until my manuscript was ready for you to work on. I'm so thankful that we got along so beautifully throughout the entire project. You're a dream to work with!

Kim Shaffer and Carol Ostercamp at United Graphics Incorporated – Although I received many bids from printing companies, I chose UGI because you made me feel so comfortable with the entire printing process. Matthew was right about your being one of the nicest guys he's ever worked with – and you are located in Terre Haute, Indiana! Another God thing! Thank you for making this such an enjoyable experience.

Paul Inbody at PK Designs – You were great at making me feel that my small project was a top priority for you. Thank you for making all the minor detail changes that I asked for on my logo. Thank you so much for your patience and working on it until it was just as I wanted it.

Thank you Jesus for being my Lord and Savior. Thank you for always being there for me, even when I'm being a fair-weather Christian. My prayer is that my writing always glorifies you. When I get off track and start writing on my own, thank you for sending me reminders that my talent comes from You – without you, my writing is dull and flat. You are my rock and my foundation! I love you.

$\mathcal{F}$*oreword*

When I first met Michelle Bailey Webster, I wanted to smack her! She was cute. She was enthusiastic. She was impatient. Michelle wanted to learn how to write a Pulitzer Price Winning Novel - and she wanted to learn it all in about fifteen minutes. Yep, she was impatient. But she was also a sponge, an eager apprentice who sought to learn all she could about the process of writing.

Though it took a little longer than fifteen minutes, *The Christmas of Miracles*, a book by Michelle Bailey Webster, is now in your hands. It is a book about a very wise child, a loving family, the pain of grief and the healing power of love. It is a book that shows angels come in all shapes and sizes and events we call "coincidence" may actually be the presence of the Divine entering our daily lives. And for Michelle, this book is proof that the dreams we hold so dear may become reality when we are enthusiastic learners who let nothing stand in our way.

There is one big difference between Michelle and many others who want help with writing and publishing. The difference? Michelle writes. She doesn't just talk about writing - she does it. In fact, the text for *The Christmas of Miracles* was written long before I ever met her. Several months ago, Shari Harvey told me, "You have to meet my sister, Michelle. She has written a book and would like to have it published. I think you can help her."

Then a few days later my friend, Lauren Biggs, told me, "You have to meet my neighbor, Michelle Webster. She has written a book and would like to have it published. I think you can help her."

Coincidence?

So we met . . . and met . . . and met. In fact, we convened every other Tuesday at a local Chili's restaurant. We sipped gallons of diet coke. We consumed burgers of all sorts and nibbled hundreds of chicken crispers. Our little booth became a labor and delivery room where the final version of *The Christmas of Miracles* was born.

Quite frankly, I was surprised when Michelle asked me to write the foreword for her book. There were times I was sure she would never speak to me again as I lectured her about verb tenses and her penchant for exclamation points.

There were times when she, no doubt, wanted to scream when I told her "this section is not working - you weren't in the 'zone' so go back and start again. There were other times I was sure she was ready to smack me when I told her, "Rewrite, rewrite, and then rewrite." Writing may be about putting words on paper but good writing is about rewriting. So Michelle, despite her impatience, did rewrite because she wanted to produce the very best book possible.

Just before our last meeting at Chili's, I received an e-mail from Michelle. She was confused, impatient and frustrated. She was convinced her book would never be a reality. Her problem? Suggestions were coming to Michelle from a wide variety of well-meaning friends and relatives. Suddenly Michelle was writing to please everyone else and lost touch with her characters and her story. I sent her a rather harsh e-mail reminding her that this story was hers and she needed to stop listening to all the voices around and learn to trust herself. And she needed to invite God to guide her as she typed each word. She wrote me back immediately and said, "Thank you. This is exactly what I needed to hear."

Boy, was I relieved. I thought she was going to smack me!

Enjoy *The Christmas of Miracles* by my friend, Michelle Bailey Webster. It celebrates the most miraculous season of the year. It reminds us that hope is greater than our past wounds and daily anxieties. It confirms that pain is an inevitable part of life, but God's grace is ever-present. Most importantly, it demonstrates the importance of simply loving one another.

As for the author, she not only has a book, Michelle Bailey Webster has realized a long-held dream and the value of learning to trust her own instincts. That's a great lesson for all of us, don't you think? (And no one ever got smacked!)

Cathy Lee Phillips
April 2004

The Christmas
of Miracles

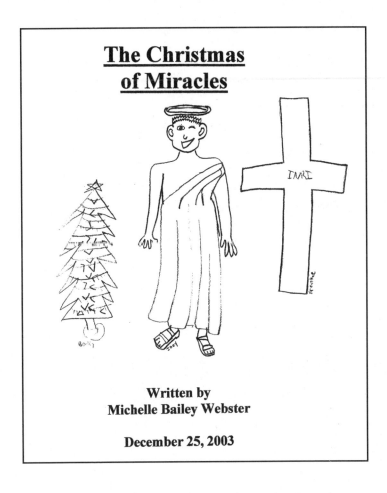

**Written by
Michelle Bailey Webster**

December 25, 2003

Original book cover design by Joey, Frankie, and Bailey Webster

The Christmas
of Miracles

✦

Chapter
ONE

Staring at the presents under the Christmas tree, Skyler Dawn fidgeted as she twirled a piece of her long, blonde curls around her finger. With just two days to go before Christmas, Skyler Dawn didn't think she would survive the anticipation of waiting to open her presents.

"Oh Pappy, can't I please open just one present?"

"Two more days, Sky, just two more days." Pappy knew how hard it must be for a four-year-old to show self-control when it came to opening presents. But he was committed to teaching Skyler Dawn that Christmas meant a whole lot more than just receiving gifts.

"Do you remember what the first gift of Christmas was?"

"I know, I know." Skyler Dawn rattled off the story as she knew it. "Mary and Joseph rode a donkey to a hotel." She gave her grandpa a confused look. "I still don't get why they didn't just go in their car."

Pappy chuckled, as Skyler Dawn continued. "The grumpy man at the hotel wouldn't let them rest in one of his rooms, so they snuck off and went to sleep with the horsies and all the other animals. In the morning, Jesus was sitting in a manger. All the animals sat around him, licking his face. A bright star was shining in the sky, and three really smart guys came by to see Jesus. Since it was Christmas, they brought him gifts."

Skyler Dawn looked at her grandfather with a very stern look on her face. Lowering her voice, she said, "They didn't make Jesus wait to open his presents!"

She continued. "They brought him gold, franks, cents, and a mirror. Poor Jesus. Those weren't very good presents. Why would anyone give a baby hot dogs for Christmas? I hope they gave him ketchup, too. Those were the first gifts of Christmas, Pappy." Skyler Dawn was standing by the Christmas tree with her hands on her hips. "Since I can't open my presents, can I go play?"

Pappy held out his arms to her, "Come here and give me a hug, you silly goose."

Skyler Dawn ran into his arms, hopped onto his lap, and wrapped her little fingers around his neck. "I love you, Pappy," then in a slight whisper, "even though you won't let me open a present." Rubbing her nose gently across Pappy's nose, she gave him a loving Eskimo kiss.

"I love you too, Baby Girl."

Reaching behind him, Pappy opened his little wooden box that held certain mementos. It contained his dog tags from the Vietnam War, money from all the different places he had been, and other sentimental items.

"Little Miss Skyler Dawn," Pappy said in his best game show host voice, "I now present you with your very first gift this Christmas."

Skyler Dawn's face lit up with excitement. "Pappyyyyy, you tricked me! Can I really open it?"

"Well…since you were able to tell me your story of the first gift of Christmas, I suppose I'll let you go ahead and open it."

Bouncing on Pappy's lap, Skyler Dawn ripped at the wrapping paper and tossed it on the floor. "What is it, Pappy? What is it?"

"You're gonna have to open it all the way to find out."

With a final rip, a beautiful manger scene emerged from its cumbersome surroundings.

"This is just what I was talking about, Pappy! See how all the animals are sitting around Jesus? And see this? It's the star I told you about. And these must be the first gifts of Christmas," Skyler Dawn said, pointing to the three wise men. "But I don't know what this is, Pappy."

"That says 1996. It tells us what year it is. That way, when you're as old as I am, you'll see this and tell your granddaughter, 'My Pappy gave this to me in 1996 when I was just 4 years old.'"

"Oh, Pappy, you're so silly! I'll never be as old as you are."

Hopping off Pappy's lap, Skyler Dawn carefully placed the ornament on one of the lower branches of the tree. There was no doubt who had decorated the Christmas tree, as most of the ornaments rested on the bottom third of the tree.

"Thank you, Pappy! Can I go play now?"

As Skyler Dawn ran out of the room, a far-away gaze filled Pappy's face. "Skyler, son, I'm gonna need your help. Your precious baby girl has no clue what Christmas is really about. If you and God could come up with a plan to help me teach her, I sure would appreciate it. Oh, one more thing, could you let me in on that plan?"

Nana Anna walked into the living room and wrapped her arms around her husband's waist. At 48 years old, she was still ravishing. Her dark hair didn't have a strand of gray in it. Her figure was every bit as good as it was when Curtis married her. The only real difference was her eyes and her smile. They were laden with pain.

"Who are you talking to, Curtis?"

Curtis knew that Anna wouldn't want to hear anything he had to say about talking to their son, Skyler. After Skyler was killed, almost 5 years before, Anna's heart slowly became hardened with bitterness. She wanted nothing to do with the God who took her son away. Curtis hoped and prayed for Anna to open her heart and accept the love and healing that can only come from Jesus Christ.

Hugging his wife, Curtis reflected, "I was just thinking about how wonderful our life is. We are so blessed to have Skyler Dawn. I wish she could have known her father, but I really believe that his short life can still be a blessing to us as well as to Skyler Dawn."

Unwrapping her arms from Curtis' waist, Anna slowly walked toward the window. She couldn't bear hearing Curtis talk about how blessed they were. Pointing to the playroom, Anna spoke in a painfully slow and monotone voice, "That little girl in there will never know her father. How can that possibly be a blessing?"

Curtis desperately wanted Anna to let go of her bitterness and recognize that God can bring good out of anything - even something as horrible as death. "Skyler Dawn may know her father in ways we will never understand," Curtis whispered gently.

Whipping her body around, Anna looked at Curtis coldly. "He's gone, Curtis. He's gone! No matter how much you dream of him, or think of him, or talk to him, he is never coming back!"

Curtis wanted to slap himself. Why couldn't he be patient and have faith in God's timing? He desperately wanted to entrust Anna to God's hands. Every time, he tried to prod God along in the matter, he only pushed Anna further from God and himself.

"I'm sorry, Honey. Can we please just forget I ever said anything and try to enjoy our Christmas holidays?"

"It would be a lot easier to enjoy the Christmas holidays if God hadn't taken our only child away from us," Anna replied bitterly.

Hurt and angry, Anna turned on her heel and stomped out of the room.

Curtis gazed upward with tears in his eyes.

"Oh, Dear God, please give me the wisdom to know when to shut my mouth. Anna is such a wonderful, loving woman underneath that tough exterior. She is still hurting so much, God. Please put a crack in that hard shell she has protecting her heart. Help her to feel your unconditional love. Bring her back to us, God."

Chapter
TWO

Skyler Dawn lived with her Mama, her Auntie Serena and her Mama's parents, Grampa Alex and Gramma Jenna. She had a very unique situation because her Daddy's parents lived right next door. She spent a lot of time going back and forth between the two houses.

While playing with her doll house at Pappy and Nana Anna's, Skyler Dawn spotted her Grampa Alex and Gramma Jenna through their kitchen window. They were standing at the sink peeling potatoes for Christmas dinner. Occasionally, Skyler Dawn would stop playing long enough to smile and wave to them. One time, she glanced up to see Gramma Jenna with potato peels draped over her nose. Grampa Alex had them hanging from his ears like earrings. Their routine had Skyler Dawn rolling on the floor, laughing hysterically.

Of course, her response to their antics only encouraged her grandparents to continue their drama. Finally, Skyler

Dawn couldn't take it anymore – she had to go over and join them in their potato peel adventure. Holding up one finger, Skyler Dawn let her grandparents know she would be over in a minute. She bounded out of the playroom.

"Nana Anna! Nana Anna!"

Skyler Dawn ran through the house until she found her grandma folding laundry in the utility room.

"Nana Anna, can I go next door, and help Grampa Alex and Gramma Jenna in the kitchen?"

"Sure, baby. Help me fold this load of laundry and I'll walk you over there."

Skyler Dawn folded the washcloths and hand towels. After a few minutes of silence, Skyler Dawn asked, "Nana Anna, do you ever think about my daddy?"

Curtis was walking into the room but stopped suddenly when he heard Skyler Dawn's question.

Nana Anna put down the shirt she was folding. She tried so hard to keep Skyler Dawn from seeing her bitterness. "Oh, Skyler Dawn, I think about him all the time – especially during the holidays."

"How come you never talk about him?" the little girl asked innocently.

Swallowing hard, Nana Anna tried to think of an answer. "Well, Sky, I guess it's because I miss him so much that it makes me sad when I talk about him."

Skyler Dawn looked serious, "I'm sorry, Nana. Ya know— he misses you too."

Nana Anna was taken aback. After a brief pause, she asked, "Why would you say that, baby?"

"Because he told me," Skyler Dawn said cautiously. "I wish you would talk about my Daddy more. When people talk about him, it makes me feel like – like he's alive – like he's really here with me."

"He is, Baby Girl. He is always with you. He's like your very own guardian angel."

Nana Anna's heart hurt for Skyler Dawn, her precious granddaughter who would never have the chance to know her own father.

Curtis smiled. He was very proud of Anna because he knew just how hard this conversation must be for her. He wondered if she really believed what she was saying to Skyler Dawn.

Skyler Dawn looked down at the washcloth she was folding, "I talk to him," she said shyly.

"I think we all do, Cutie."

"Yeah," Skyler Dawn was hesitant, but kept talking. "Nana," she said softly, "he talks to me, too."

Stunned, Anna had no idea how to respond. She remembered that Curtis had said the same thing to her shortly after Skyler died. Anna told him harshly that he was imagining things. After that, he never broached the subject again. But Anna often wondered if Curtis still thought he heard Skyler speaking to him. Though she wasn't comfortable with the conversation she was having with Skyler Dawn, she didn't want to push her away as she had Curtis.

"What does he say?"

"It just depends. Ya know when I had my tonsils out?"

"Yeah"

"Well, he went into the operating room with me and held my hand until I fell asleep. When I woke up, he was still holding my hand and singing to me."

"What was he singing?"

"I don't know. It was the first time I'd ever heard that song. But every once in a while when I can't fall asleep, he'll come into my room, tickle my back and sing the same song to me."

"Do you remember how it goes?"

"It starts with the word sunshine. Daddy says that I'm his sunshine!"

Anna's face went white. The song, *Sunshine on my Shoulders*, by John Denver, was quite popular in the mid 70's, as the Vietnam War was coming to a close. It gave

Americans hope during a very tumultuous time. Curtis had been a Vietnam POW for a little over a year. On March 29th, 1973 he was finally released along with 590 other POW's. Thin and malnourished, Curtis was in poor physical condition, carrying the emotional scars that never leave a prisoner of war.

Although Curtis and Anna were sweethearts before the war, Curtis wanted nothing to do with Anna when he first returned home. It was not until the end of July that he finally broke down the barriers and started seeing Anna again. They married that Christmas. In the fall of the following year, Skyler was born. From the moment Anna found out she was expecting, she sang that song to her growing belly. It was the first song Skyler ever learned.

Anna needed time to let Skyler Dawn's comments sink in. She set the clothes basket down on the floor and stood up.

"Okay Cutie, are you ready to go see your other grandparents?"

Skyler Dawn threw down the washcloth she was folding, "Oh yeah - I almost forgot. Let's go!"

Curtis tiptoed back to the living room and stood beside the Christmas tree. Once he saw Anna and Skyler Dawn walking next door, he collapsed to his knees. "Thank you God! Thank you, thank you, thank you. And Skyler, I see you and the Big Guy are working hard up there. I suppose if anyone could help put a crack in that rigid outer shell of your Mama's, it would be that little girl of yours. Keep up the good work!"

Skyler Dawn burst through her grandparent's kitchen door, full of enthusiasm. "CUTIE'S HERE!" she announced.

"Well c'mon over here, Cutie. I need some help mashing up all these potatoes," Gramma Jenna said, handing her a potato masher.

"Oh no you don't," said Grampa Alex, "not until she helps me put the glaze on this ham."

Anna, meanwhile, went back home through her back door, heading straight for the bedroom to lie down. She didn't want to see or talk to Curtis right now. She just wanted to close her eyes and reflect on her conversation with Skyler Dawn.

Chapter
THREE

"Have you decided yet what you are going to get Skyler Dawn from Skyler this year?" Serena asked her twin sister, Melina.

Skyler had been killed in a freak accident before Melina even knew she was pregnant. Every year, Melina tried to get something special for Skyler Dawn that would help her feel connected to her daddy. The paradox was that sometimes it seemed as though Skyler Dawn had a connection with her Daddy that transcended human relationships.

"You know that song I told you I keep hearing in my head?" Melina asked Serena.

"I think so. You can't remember the title or why it's stuck in your head, right?"

"That's the one."

"What about it?" Serena wondered what that had to do with Skyler Dawn's Christmas present.

"Well, last night I had a dream that Skyler was singing that song to Skyler Dawn."

"The exact same song?"

Melina nodded her head.

"Were you able to figure out the name of the song?" Serena knew this song had really been weighing heavily on Melina's heart. They both believed it had some sort of significance, though neither one of them knew what that was.

Melina continued talking, not even hearing what Serena had asked her. "It was an incredible dream. Everything was in color and so vivid. If I didn't know that Skyler was dead, I would swear this actually happened."

"Don't keep me in suspense! What happened?"

"In the dream, we were in Skyler Dawn's bedroom. She was sleeping in her canopy bed. The white Victorian lace on her windows barely shaded the morning sun. It was like I was looking through the lens of a camera. Then the camera panned over to the wall and I could see a man's shadow kneeling next to Skyler Dawn's bed."

"Was it Skyler?"

"I didn't know at first. But I could tell that whoever it was, wasn't there to harm Skyler Dawn. In fact, I felt encompassed by the love that filled her room. Finally the camera panned back to the bed and there was Skyler leaning next to Skyler Dawn's bed. He was brushing her hair away from her face and talking to her. It was as though he had never been gone."

"So, you actually saw Skyler in the dream?"

"Yes! I am absolutely positive it was Skyler. He looked exactly like he did when he was alive."

"Have you ever seen him like that in a dream before?"

"No – not like this! I've felt him and I've heard him. I've even seen shadows and outlines of him. But I've never seen him up close. Serena, I looked into his blue eyes. They sparkled with his love for Skyler Dawn. I saw every wrinkle on his knuckles as he stroked Skyler Dawn's face. I actually saw his fingernails." Melina laughed. "He had a little dirt under them, and they needed to be trimmed. I swear, Serena, it was like he was really there."

Melina was so thankful for her twin sister. Serena was the only person she could share such intimate thoughts regarding a dream like this. Anyone else might think she had lost her mind.

"Did he say anything to Skyler Dawn?"

"Yeah, Skyler Dawn was looking straight into his eyes the way a daughter looks at her daddy. It was incredible. I could see in her eyes how much she loved him. You aren't going to believe what he did while he was humming that song to her. He took his index finger and wrapped the curls on her forehead around it, twirling her hair just like she does.

"After a couple of minutes, Skyler Dawn asked, 'Daddy, what are you singing?' Skyler paused for a second, but didn't answer the question."

"Oh my gosh. Please tell me he told her the name of the song," Serena interjected.

"No. Instead he asked her, 'Do you know how much your mama and I love you?'"

Serena grabbed the tissues off the bedside table giving one to Melina and taking one for herself. "What did Skyler Dawn say?"

Melina blew her nose and wiped the tears from her eyes.

"Skyler Dawn said, 'Of course I do, Daddy. You tell me all the time. You love me from here to eternity and back again.'"

"Skyler spoke to her, 'That's right, baby girl. But do you remember who loves you even more than your mommy and I do?'"

Sniffling, Serena grabbed another tissue.

Melina talked as if she were in another time and place. "Skyler Dawn said, 'Daddddddeeeeee – you always ask me that. God does, of course.'

"Skyler gazed at her, his eyes filled with love and tenderness. Holding her face between his hands, he said,

'That's right, baby, that's right.' Then he hummed that same song again. He tickled her back until she was asleep, kissed her on the forehead and whispered, 'Goodnight, Sunshine.' Then he stood up and looked at me. Serena, I swear he looked directly into my eyes."

"Did he say anything?" Serena asked.

"No, he just nodded slowly and gave me a wink. It was like he was saying, 'I'm still here baby. I'll never leave you and Skyler Dawn.' Then he slowly faded into the distance."

Serena was speechless. She waited to see if Melina was going to say anything else. When it was clear that Melina had finished talking, Serena blurted, "Wow! That sounds so real. How did you feel afterward?"

"It was really weird. When I woke up, for a split second, I thought the dream was real. It was as if Skyler was alive and we were raising Skyler Dawn together. It felt like we were a real family. Then reality set in. Although I felt a sense of peace, my heart ached - longing for him to be here. He would have been such a great father."

Melina paused, trying to keep her composure. "Oh Serena, I just miss him so much. I want him here with me. I want him to hold me in his arms - not just wink at me in a dream. I want his daughter to know him personally, instead of just hearing stories about him. I want us to be a family!"

Melina finally broke down. Serena wrapped her arms around Melina. "I'm sorry, Mel. I'm so sorry."

"It's always a little tougher around the holidays."

"I know, Melina, I know," Serena rocked back and forth with Melina as though she were a small child.

"You know, I came to terms with his death a long time ago. But then something happens - like this dream - and it brings back all the pain of losing him. In my head, I know God has a different plan for my life. But in my heart, I want Skyler here – with Skyler Dawn and me.

"I've got to tell you, Serena, Anna's bitterness does not help! Her anger hurts all of us during the holidays. The fact that we can't even mention Skyler's name in front of her is just plain selfish. She is thinking of no one but herself and her pain. Skyler Dawn is going to catch on pretty soon that talking about her daddy in front of his own mother is a big taboo. That is not right. Anna needs to get help or learn to deal with it - if for no other reason, than for the sake of her granddaughter."

"We just need to keep praying for her, Mel. She'll come around in time."

"In time? Serena, it's been almost five years! If she hasn't come around by now, she's never going to."

"Remember, Mel, God can soften even the hardest of hearts."

"I know – but I sure wish He'd hurry up." Melina laughed halfheartedly at her own impatience. "I know God's will and timing are better than my own, but I still want Him to do things *my* way, when *I* want them done."

"I know, Sis. I know," Serena said softly.

✧ *Michelle Bailey Webster* ✧

Chapter
FOUR

Christmas Eve finally arrived. This was the day Pappy promised to take Skyler Dawn shopping to buy a special present for her mommy.

Sitting Indian style at the kitchen window, Skyler Dawn's elbows were propped on her knees with her cheeks settled into the palms of each hand. Waiting for Pappy to come over was almost as hard as waiting to open presents. Pappy kept his own schedule, staying up late in the evenings, then sleeping until morning was almost over. Skyler Dawn wasn't allowed to go over to her other grandparent's house until she could see Pappy through the kitchen window enjoying his morning coffee.

This morning, Skyler Dawn had been ready and waiting anxiously for nearly two hours. At ten minutes before eleven, she finally saw Pappy shuffling up the sidewalk. "Pappy's here! Pappy's here! Bye-bye Mama. Bye-bye Auntie Serena."

Melina and Serena were busy fixing their famous

pumpkin and pecan pies. "Get over here, Baby Girl, and give Mama a kiss."

Skyler Dawn rushed over to her mama. Melina bent over, kissed her on the cheek, and dabbed a bit of flour on the end of Skyler Dawn's nose. "Bye, Baby Girl. You be good for your Pappy."

"I will Mama. Bye bye." When Skyler Dawn bounded into her Pappy's arms, he flung her onto his back for a piggyback ride. The ringlets in her blonde pigtails bounced up and down as Pappy galloped to the car.

"Well Cutie – have you thought about what you want to get your mama this year?"

Skyler Dawn was quiet for a moment. Shyly she asked, "Pappy, you know who I really want to get something special for?"

"Who do you really want to get something special for?" Pappy asked, mimicking her.

"I wanna get something special for Nana Anna this year. I think she's sad. Yesterday, I asked her why she never talks about my daddy. She seemed really sad when I asked her that. I didn't mean to make Nana Anna sad, so I wanna get her something that will make her feel happy again."

Pappy choked back the lump that formed in the back of his throat. "You know, Sky, you didn't make Nana Anna sad.

She always gets sad around Christmas because she misses your daddy. She wishes he could be here with us."

Skyler Dawn's tears started flowing down her chubby little cheeks. "Yeah, I guess so, but I still think I made her sad."

Skyler Dawn was much too wise for her four short years. "I know it feels that way, Sky, but I promise, you did NOT make Nana Anna sad." What he really wanted to say was that Nana Anna hadn't been happy for five years.

Skyler Dawn's smile started emerging, "I still wanna buy her a special present."

"That sounds wonderful. I think Nana Anna would like that very much."

"But I wanna get something for Mama, too!"

Around Thanksgiving, Skyler Dawn began begging Grampa Alex and Gramma Jenna for extra chores to earn money for Christmas presents. But even though Skyler Dawn brought her own money, Pappy was more than willing to slip in a few extra dollars so she could buy presents for both her Mama and Nana Anna.

Pappy laughed. "Baby Girl – I'm sure you'll be able to get something for Nana Anna and your Mama."

Chapter
FIVE

Once Anna heard Curtis' truck pull out of the driveway she dragged herself out of bed. She had tossed and turned all night after her conversation with Skyler Dawn. She could not get out of her mind what Skyler Dawn had said about her daddy singing to her and calling her "Sunshine."

Anna went over to her bookshelves and stared at the dusty, brown journal sitting next to the old Bible she once read so fervently. She used to talk to God through her journal almost every day. But after Skyler died she had a hard time writing. Anna wasn't angry with God at first. She was just overwhelmingly sad. And it seemed no matter how hard she prayed, she simply could not find the God she had loved since she was a small child.

Though time passed, she just couldn't recover from the pain of losing her only child. That is when she decided that the God she thought would always be there for her didn't exist after all. But now she was beginning to wonder again. Was He actually trying to reach out to her through Curtis and Skyler Dawn? Anna finally gathered the courage to slide the journal off the shelf. With the journal tucked close to her chest, she got back in bed. She propped her pillows against the headboard and curled up beneath the down comforter that adorned her bed. Slowly, Anna opened the journal. Flipping through it, Anna looked at the months following Skyler's death, finally stopping at the last entry.

May 6, 1992

The tears that fall
Are left untouched.
No matter how far I run,
They follow me,
Like my shadow.
Never leaving.
Never giving me a moment of peace.
I hide in the corner,
Rolled up in a ball.

Why, God, why?
Why couldn't you have taken me instead?
How do I go on?
I can't find you God.

Please show me you're here.
Where do I go?
How do I find You?
I need a roadmap,
An outline.

How do I open my heart?
How do I let You in?

God, fill my heart,
Overflow my soul.
Please catch my tears.
Free me from my pain.

I don't feel your love.
Are you there, God?
Are you really there?

After Anna wrote this journal entry, she gave up. She was convinced she would never feel better again. She quit asking for God's help. Her pain turned into anger and eventually to bitterness. Throwing her journal across the room, Anna curled up in a ball, weeping as she rocked painfully in the center of her bed.

After what seemed like an eternity, Anna cried out in anguish, "GOD, IF YOU ARE THERE, I NEED TO KNOW. PLEASE SOMEHOW LET ME KNOW. SEND ME A HUGE SIGN!" Anna sobbed into her pillow, "I need a sign. Please God, just give me a sign."

Chapter
SIX

Once the pies were finished baking, Melina and Serena went shopping for that special Christmas present for Skyler Dawn. They first went to a specialty store in the 'Shops of Dunwoody' called *Sonkist Doves*. The store was run by a Christian family who had lived in Dunwoody when it was just a few houses spread thinly amid vast acres of woods. Now Dunwoody is a rapidly growing suburb of Atlanta. The owners wanted to open a bookstore carrying unique items reflecting their spiritual beliefs. This was not your typical Christian bookstore.

Last year at *Sonkist Doves,* Melina found a crystal dove with a gorgeous crystal rainbow behind it. Melina told Skyler Dawn that the dove was like her prayers, being carried on a rainbow from earth to heaven. Melina thought it a beautiful reminder that God and her Daddy are just a prayer away. Skyler Dawn kept the piece on her bedside table with a picture of herself next to the dove and a picture of her daddy on the other side of the rainbow.

This year Melina had only a vague idea of what she wanted to buy for Skyler Dawn. Although *Sonkist Doves* had some really distinctive items, as soon as she walked through the front door Melina knew that Skyler Dawn's present wasn't there.

"Why don't we try one of the shops in Olde Roswell?" Serena suggested.

Olde Roswell is a square of unique shops and thrift stores in the heart of Roswell, Georgia, a few miles due north of downtown Atlanta. The Victorian shops look as though they came right out of the twenties - vintage lace, dolls and antiques. There are several restaurants including a dainty, little tearoom often used for wedding and baby showers. Occasionally, Nana Anna, Gramma Jenna, Melina, and Serena would bring Skyler Dawn to high tea to practice their good, old-fashioned southern manners.

"That's a good idea. If I'm going to find it anywhere, it will probably be in Olde Roswell."

Strolling through the square of Olde Roswell, they happened upon a quaint boutique called *The Little Shop of Antiques.* Although the store looked a bit pretentious from the outside, Melina could see a large three tiered table in the middle of the room covered with angels and music boxes.

"I think this is it!" Melina's eyes danced with excitement as she approached the front entrance. Heading straight toward the center table, she carefully studied each angel and music box.

"These are stunning. Skyler Dawn would love any of these. Do you see what you are looking for?" Serena asked.

Before Melina could answer, a saleslady appeared from the back room. She had her coal-black hair pulled back in a tight bun and wore round, silver glasses. She looked like a librarian. Her bun was so severe that she had no wrinkles around her hairline and her eyebrows were pulled halfway up her forehead. She wore bright red lipstick, which only emphasized her pale, stern face. Approaching Melina and Serena with her sharp nose held high in the air and her lips pursed, she haughtily asked, "May I help you?"

Hoping this woman wasn't as snooty as she appeared, Melina responded cheerfully. "I hope so. I am looking for something very special for my daughter."

"Oh, how old is your daughter?" the saleswoman asked in a condescending tone.

"She is a very mature four."

"Miss, I can assure you there is nothing here that would be appropriate for your four-year-old daughter. As you can see, everything we carry in this store is very delicate – and quite expensive. No doubt, you see that we cater to a very select group of people." With a pompous laugh, the saleswoman continued, "I am certain that your daughter does not fit in that class."

Put off by her pretentious attitude, purchasing a present for Skyler Dawn from this store was no longer an option for Melina.

Serena didn't even have to see the look on Melina's face to know they were finished at this store. She knew she had better step in quick to diffuse the situation. Looking at the woman with all the kindness she could muster, Serena said, "You are probably right. We will try somewhere else. Thank you."

Melina grumbled, venting her anger as they walked from the store and into the parking lot. Putting her arm around her sister, Serena muttered, "I guess it wouldn't be Christmas if we didn't run across a scrooge."

Both women noticed a very striking, petite woman who had followed them out of the shop. Not quite 5 feet tall, she probably weighed less than 95 pounds. She looked to be in her late 60's or early70's. Her hair, a perfect silver, framed her soft oval face. As the woman walked past the girls, Melina noticed that she smelled of the same fragrance as her own grandmother – *Jean Naté, After Bath Splash*.

This woman was very modern and trendy for her age. Her brown and beige suit looked as though it came straight out of a Lord and Taylor catalogue. She wore brown snakeskin shoes and carried a matching handbag. This striking woman had a presence the twins couldn't help but admire. "I hope when I'm her age, I carry myself with that kind of poise and dignity," Melina whispered. Both girls watched her as the woman walked toward her brown 1997 Lincoln Continental.

Anxious to complete their shopping so they could get home and finish the Christmas preparations, Serena encouraged Melina to move on.

"Where to next?"

"Let's just start walking around the square. I'm sure we'll find something," Melina said.

"Excuse me, Miss," the older woman said walking toward Melina carrying a pink box about six inches square.

Melina turned cautiously.

"I'm sorry to bother you but I couldn't help but overhear your conversation with the salesperson in there." The petite woman spoke with a lovely British accent.

"I have a very special item that I had arranged to sell to the owner of *The Little Shop of Antiques*. The woman pulled from the box an odd shaped object carefully wrapped in pink polka dot tissue paper. "As I witnessed the way she treated you, I knew this piece was much too precious for me to sell to someone who isn't respectful of her own clientele. I noticed that you were looking at the presentation of angels and music boxes. I believe that I might have the perfect gift for your four-year-old daughter."

Though pressed for time, Melina hid her anxiety and agreed to look at the item.

Carefully removing the first piece of tissue paper, the woman spoke. "This angel was handcrafted by my son, Adrian Saunders, when he was in his late teens. He made three of them. One for me, one for his wife, and one for his daughter. The one that he made for his daughter was also a music box - that was the only angel he ever created with a music box inside. He was an incredibly gifted stone sculptor. He could create almost anything out of a chunk of stone."

The woman pulled away the last piece of tissue paper. A precious angel emerged from the pink paper clouds. It was the most beautiful angel Melina or Serena had ever seen.

"Adrian made this angel from a mineral called jadeite. It is a form of jade. It is very rare to find a pink piece of jadeite large enough to sculpt into anything other than jewelry.

"When most people sculpt angels, they sculpt female angels, but the first three angels Adrian sculpted were all male angels."

"May I hold it?" Melina was incredibly drawn to the angel.

The woman held out the pink angel. Cupping the angel in her hands, Melina felt a peace-like tingle flow from the tips of her fingers then spread through the rest of her body.

Melina caressed each tiny groove on the angel sculpture. "This is amazing." Awestruck, Melina's voice came out in breathy whispers. "I have never seen anything more stunning than this lovely angel."

Melina looked back at the woman, "I was actually looking for a music box, but this angel is the exact replica of the angel that I had pictured in my head. I envisioned a male angel, with extra small wings, winking with his left eye. I can't help but wonder though why you would want to sell something so precious to you."

The woman stared at her feet for nearly a minute before she spoke. When she finally looked up, a tear trickled down her cheek. "It's a long story, but it's a beautiful one. If you have the time to hear it, we could go next door to the Tea Room and I'll tell you a little tale."

Chapter
SEVEN

Pappy and Skyler Dawn walked back and forth along the entire lower level of the mall. Pappy really didn't care where they went or how long it took. He just enjoyed any opportunity to spend time alone with his granddaughter.

Skyler Dawn, however, darted in and out of the stores with purpose. She finally looked at Pappy dejectedly, "I just don't see what I want to get for Mama or Nana Anna. What if I don't find anything? Christmas is tomorrow!"

"Come on, Cutie, we haven't even looked on the upper level. I'm sure you'll find something there."

Skyler Dawn didn't feel as optimistic. In fact, if her head hung any lower, she would have stepped on it. Pappy led her to the escalator so she wouldn't bump in to anything.

As soon as they got to the top of the escalator, Skyler Dawn peeked up through her blonde curls and saw a kiosk full of music boxes.

"That's it, Pappy, that's it! That's exactly what I'm looking for!"

Pappy was looking at the kiosk selling Georgia peach jellies and jams. "You've been looking for jelly all this time?" he asked incredulously.

Skyler Dawn looked at Pappy sideways and laughed, "Not there, Pappy. Over here. C'mon."

Skyler Dawn raced to the kiosk, challenging Pappy to keep up with her. She instinctively reached for the music boxes, caressing and scrutinizing each one. Pappy refrained from stopping her when he saw how cautiously Skyler Dawn handled the fragile items.

Skyler Dawn eyed one in the back that she couldn't reach. "Pappy, see that one way back there behind the nutcracker? The clear one?"

Pappy pointed to a crystal angel in the very back. "This one?" Skyler Dawn nodded her head enthusiastically. Pappy reached behind all the other music boxes and grasped the crystal angel. He very carefully placed it in Skyler Dawn's hands.

Oh, Pappy, this is it! This is what I want to buy for Nana Anna."

The man who worked at the kiosk walked over to Pappy and Skyler Dawn.

"Hello there, Li'l Miss." He bent down on one knee to be closer to Skyler Dawn's height.

Because Skyler Dawn spent so much time with grownups, she spoke with them as if she were an adult herself. "I want to buy this angel for my Nana Anna for Christmas."

"It's a beautiful angel, but turn it over, sweetheart. One of the wings is broken off and the music box doesn't even work. Why don't I help you find something better for your Nana Anna? We'll find one that is perfect."

Skyler Dawn eyed him with disappointment. "But I don't want another one. I want this one," she said quietly.

The gentleman stood up to speak to Pappy. "This crystal angel arrived without an invoice in one of our shipments from Washington D.C. We haven't figured out what to do with it. I don't even know why it is on this shelf. Every time I see it on the shelf, I move it to a box underneath the cart, but somehow it keeps reappearing on the shelf.

"Sir, we've had our technician try unsuccessfully to get this music box to play. Evidently, the angel was immersed in water for an extended period of time, rusting the interior music box. When trying to remove the defective music box, one of the angels' wings broke off."

"Considering that the crystal wing and the music box are both broken, how much are you willing to sell it for?" Pappy wanted to know.

The man thought for a second, "We've sanded down the sharp edges, so I'm not concerned about your little girl getting cut…Honestly, you'd be doing me a favor if you just took it. We can't sell it and I can't bear to throw it out, but the way it keeps appearing on my shelf is driving me nuts. My wife and I are the only ones who work this cart and she has been having the same problem."

The gentleman looked at Skyler Dawn, "Here you go, Li'l Miss. I want you to have this angel," the gentleman said handing the angel to Skyler Dawn.

As Skyler Dawn looked down at her feet, a tear fell out of her right eye, landing on her shiny, black Mary Jane's. Presenting the angel back to the gentleman, Skyler Dawn said, "I don't want you to give this to me."

Confused, the gentleman asked, "Why not? This is a gift from me to you."

Skyler Dawn's blue eyes sparkled with tears. "Because, this is for my Nana Anna. I made her sad yesterday. I really want to buy something special for her with my own money. I did extra chores so I would have enough money to buy her a special Christmas present." Skyler Dawn burst forth with emotion. "I don't want to just give her something that someone else wants to throw away. She's much too special for that. She's my Nana Anna!"

A crowd was gathering around Skyler Dawn and the gentleman.

Pappy blinked back the tears that were forming in his eyes.

The gentleman was at a loss for words. He just looked at Skyler Dawn and the tiny little pink purse she had draped around her neck and shoulder. Realizing the magnitude of his blunder, he knelt down so he could talk to Skyler Dawn at her eye level. The gentleman held the angel towards Skyler Dawn. "Do you like this angel?" he asked her.

Skyler Dawn spoke with passion. "Oh, yes sir! I think this angel is just perfect for my Nana Anna." Skyler Dawn still had tears running down her cheeks.

"What is it about this angel that you like so much?" the gentleman wondered.

"Everything!" Skyler Dawn ran her fingers over the broken wing of the angel. "This angel looks just like my daddy. He is in heaven. He winks at me just like this angel is winking at me."

The gentleman's voice cracked. "What about the wings? Do you care that one of them is broken?" Onlookers of all ages listened intently to their conversation.

"Oh no. That is part of what makes him so perfect. You see, my daddy died before I was born. And I think when he died, it broke my Nana's heart just like this angel is broken. This angel is perfect for Nana Anna."

There were sniffles all around. Before the gentleman could even attempt to sell this defective music box to this small, yet wise child, he had to make sure she understood that the wing wasn't the only thing broken.

"What about the music box? You realize it will never play music, right?"

Skyler Dawn looked at him with complete sincerity. She lowered her eyes to the angel and smiled at it, "The right person will be able to fix this angel. And if no one else hears it, that's okay…My Daddy sings to me but I'm the only one who hears him. Just because no one hears it doesn't mean it isn't making music. I'll be able to hear it because my daddy taught me to listen with my heart…not my ears."

A tear ran down the salesman's face. "Li'l Miss, you taught me something very important today. And you are right – this music box does not deserve to be thrown away. It just needs to go to the right person."

Skyler Dawn smiled enthusiastically. "That's me! I'm the right person!"

The gentleman looked at her seriously. "Will you take extra special care of this music box?"

"Oh, yes sir."

"Will you give your Nana extra hugs and kisses on Christmas?"

"Of course I will." Skyler Dawn looked at this man with pure, selfless love flowing from her sky blue eyes.

"Just one more thing," the gentleman said, sounding very professional. "I need to make sure you have enough money to buy this beautiful masterpiece. How much do you have?"

Skyler Dawn took her pink purse off her shoulder. "I just counted it this morning. I have four dollars and forty-eight cents. Is that enough?"

Two pennies rolled across the floor and landed at Skyler Dawn's feet. She picked them up and looked around, wondering where they came from. "Li'l Miss, this is your lucky day. That music box is exactly four dollars and fifty cents. With those two pennies, you have just the right amount of money to buy this angel."

Everyone broke into applause. Completely unaware of the audience that had gathered around them, Skyler Dawn's focus remained on this imperfect, yet perfect angel. She believed it would be the one thing that could make Nana Anna feel better this Christmas season.

Many people left the shopping mall that Christmas Eve thankful for that little girl who showed them that giving selfless love was really the true meaning of Christmas.

Chapter
EIGHT

Once Anna regained some semblance of composure, she grabbed her purse, ran to her car, and started driving aimlessly. Turning on the radio, she tried to drown out the confusing thoughts spiraling through her head. Her attention was immediately directed to a news bulletin being aired.

Early Saturday afternoon, a Caucasian man, approximately 25 years of age, 6' 1" tall with dark brown hair, was discovered near death on a bench at the Five Points MARTA rail station. He was found barefoot, without a hat or coat. He carried no form of identification. He was taken via ambulance to Piedmont Hospital where he is now listed in stable condition. If anyone has any information about this man, please contact Piedmont Hospital.

Anna was familiar with Atlanta's bus and rail system called MARTA, Metro Atlanta Rapid Transit Authority. Different types of people utilize this public transportation system. Some are white-collar businesspersons who work downtown and do not want to fight Atlanta traffic. Others are blue-collar workers who probably have no other form of transportation. These individuals would obviously have a clear destination and their employers or coworkers would know if they didn't show up for work.

But it seemed that no one was looking for this man. So Anna wondered if this man was one of the poor or homeless who manage to gather enough fare money to ride the MARTA rails for a warm place to rest. Or perhaps he was an out-of-towner who might ride MARTA to visit the tourist sites or just for an adventure. The fact that he was found with no i.d. caused an endless set of questions to churn through Anna's mind. How long had he been gone? Were his family and friends aware of his disappearance? Was he a homeless Atlanta man who might never be missed or an out-of-towner who was possibly mugged? Did he have a family somewhere mourning his disappearance right now? Anna felt an instant pang for this man and those who loved him.

Switching radio stations, Anna hoped to find something to distract her from her own pain. But the same story was being broadcast on the second radio station as well. Anna changed stations a total of six times – each time hearing the identical story. How could it possibly be that all six radio stations were simultaneously airing the same news story?

Turning off her radio, Anna pulled into a coffee shop. "Okay, God. What was that about? I don't want to think about Skyler right now and I certainly don't want to think about some strange man lying in a hospital bed. If this is your way of sending me a sign, I don't see how it relates to me or my situation. I don't even want to feel my own pain, let alone someone else's. I just want to escape."

Feeling lonely and depressed, Anna meandered into the coffee shop and slumped into the only booth available.

"Here's a complementary newspaper for you, Ma'am. May I get you a cup of coffee?" When Anna didn't respond, the waitress brought a fresh pot over and sat it on the table next to the cream and sugar.

Several minutes went by before Anna looked up, noticing the newspaper and coffee pot. A bead of sweat dropped from Anna's brow when she read the front-page headlines.

Mystery Man Found Near Death At Marta Station. Anna tried to ignore the growing discomfort settling in the pit of her stomach. Rolling her eyes, she tried to push the "coincidence" out of her head. Trembling, Anna poured herself a cup of coffee and tossed the newspaper beneath the booth.

Anna looked around the restaurant hoping to distract herself from the man who seemed to be invading her every thought. Refusing to let her thoughts take over her mind, Anna read the framed quotations posted around the restaurant.

Face what you are handed. Don't hand back what you are faced with –Joseph Jameson

One who runs can never hide. One who hides will always run – Frances Eil

Helping others helps yourself more than others. – Bailey Jordan

If you are called to solve a mystery, but choose not to, who will? – Katherine Margrace.

Though you have made me see troubles, many and bitter, you will restore my life again; from the depths of the earth you will again bring me up. You will increase my honor and comfort me once again. Psalm 71:20,21

If Anna wasn't feeling so overwhelmed by all the messages that were bombarding her, she would have thought the situation comical.

Interrupting her myriad thoughts was a curly, blonde headed kid, about 20 years old, walking to the jukebox. He poured over the many different song choices for about five minutes before finally putting his money in the coin collector. Leaving the jukebox, the kid walked past Anna and said "Hello" with a kind wink and nod of his head. Stunned by the resemblance this kid had to Skyler, Anna spilled her coffee.

The culmination of events finally broke her resilience. A lonely ache soared through Anna's body. She missed Skyler with every ounce of her being. Anna swallowed the sobs that were threatening to erupt from her throat.

Regaining her composure, Anna took another sip of her coffee. The jukebox played its first selection – the Beatles singing, *Anna, Go To Him*. Anna's coffee cup slipped out of her hands shattering on the floor beneath her. Flustered, she jumped from her booth.

Anna dashed frantically from table to table looking for the kid who played that song on the jukebox.

"Did you see that kid? The blonde guy who just left the jukebox? Did you see who played that song? Where is he? Where did he go?" Anna looked into the crowd of confused faces.

Everything was silent to Anna. Men, women, children and even waitresses shook their heads and mouthed, 'noooooooo' in slow motion.

Anna ran past a small boy and his grandfather coming out of the men's bathroom. She burst through the door hoping to find the blonde, young man who played that song. The bathroom was empty.

Anna collapsed to the floor. Her loud sobs echoed off the bathroom walls. Her brown, shoulder length hair covered her face.

"GOD, WHAT ARE YOU TRYING TO DO TO ME?" Anna spewed. "Are you trying to make me crazy? What do you want from me? Please, no more signs. I'm sorry I asked for that. Don't send me anymore signs… please." Anna's shoulders heaved as loud sobs burst forth from deep within her.

"Are you okay, Ma'am?" A small voice spoke from the crowd of onlookers that had gathered around the bathroom door.

Anna's eyes darted around.

"Let us help you." Two strangers came forth and helped Anna to her feet. Everything else seemed to disappear as these two men, dressed in solid white, walked her from the coffee shop to her car. As quickly as the two men vanished, Anna's anguish seemed to disappear - only to be replenished with the prevailing clarity of what she had to do.

Chapter
NINE

"My name is Angela Saunders." The woman with the pink jadeite angel leaned forward giving Melina and Serena a kiss on both cheeks.

"Very pleased to meet you, Ms. Saunders. I'm Melina and this is my sister Serena."

Even though there were people waiting at The Tea Room, Melina, Serena, and Angela were seated immediately.

Angela was the first to speak. "My tale begins nearly half a century ago when I met my husband while training for the 1946 World Championship Equestrian Competition. He was such a gentleman. I was immediately attracted to how gentle and kind he was with his horse. People called him *Magic Jack* because of the supernatural connection he had with horses. The second I laid eyes on him, I looked at my girlfriend and said, 'I'm going to marry him.'

"Six months later we were married and making plans for our own Equestrian Center. Ten years after that we were training Olympic hopefuls at Saunders Equicentre while baby Adrian lay in a basket on the edge of the ring. He found his way into the saddle before becoming steady on his own two feet. Like his father, Adrian was born with a natural connection to the horses. As he grew older, he turned into an excellent rider and an even better trainer. But with time and circumstances, he discovered that his true passion lie in sculpting.

"As an adult, Adrian's sculpting abilities became legendary. The first thing he ever sculpted was an angel. Several times he tried sculpting other things but he found that he had an exceptional talent for sculpting angels. He believed that God had called him to sculpt angels for people in need of healing. People came from all across the world sharing their pain with Adrian. Adrian would pray with them for healing and ask God to guide him in the sculpting of their angel. His prayer always included the verse Isaiah 41:13: *For I am the Lord, your God, who takes hold of your right hand and says to you, Do not fear; I will help you.*

The angels he created always held a subtle aura.

"When Adrian was in high school. He had a delightful sweetheart named Elysia. She was a beautiful girl both inside and out. She was dark complected, had deep brownish-black eyes and silky, black hair that flowed all the way down her back. She was a sharp contrast to Adrian's fair skin, blonde, wavy hair and green eyes. They were very much in love and planned to marry one day.

"Elysia wasn't originally from Scotland. She and her father moved to Aberdeen from Spain so Elysia could train at our equestrian school. She was an exquisite rider. She probably would have been very successful competing internationally, had things turned out differently for her.

"Elysia helped at the stables in exchange for lessons. She and Adrian worked many long hours cleaning the stables and taking care of the horses. Through the years, their friendship matured into a profound love for each other.

"Elysia's father was completely opposed to their relationship. I'm sure you are both aware of the religious wars that have gone on for centuries in the European countries between the Catholics and the Protestants. Well, Spain and Scotland were deep-seated adversaries. Our family cherished our faith as believers in Jesus Christ. We loved Elysia, so it didn't matter to us that she was being raised in a different Christian denomination. She had a strong faith and the love she had for our son was unmistakable.

"We felt that Elysia was part of our family long before she and Adrian ever fell in love with each other. Sadly, Elysia's father never took the chance to get to know Adrian. Her father wouldn't even allow her to discuss their relationship, much less permit him to join her in their home. His refusal to acknowledge their relationship created an unspoken barrier between Elysia and her father. He allowed her to continue training, but thrust many more rules upon her.

"When Elysia learned she was pregnant just two months before their graduation, she first shared her news with Adrian – then together they came to Jack and me.

"Adrian was ecstatic. He wanted to marry Elysia immediately. In those days, people married much younger than they do now. We encouraged them both to wait so we could go with them to tell Elysia's father. We hoped that if we were there, we could help him understand the depth of their love for each other. Ultimately, we hoped he would give Adrian and Elysia his blessing to marry.

"Elysia was quite afraid to tell him, even with us going with her. She feared that when he found out she was pregnant, he would do something that would make it impossible for her to ever see Adrian again."

"Thank God Elysia had someone like you and your husband she could talk to. I can't imagine not being able to share with my own father about the man I love," Melina said aloud.

"Yes, it was very difficult. We arranged to bring Elysia home from her lesson on Friday evening when her father would be there. But that morning, Elysia never showed up at school. Adrian was so concerned for her that he left school and went straight to her house. When Elysia's father opened the door, Adrian knew immediately he had discovered her pregnancy. Adrian begged and pleaded with Elysia's father to allow him to see Elysia. He looked at Adrian with pure hatred and said coldly, 'She does not live here anymore. You disgraced her.' He spat at Adrian's feet and slammed the door behind him.

"Adrian dropped to the ground in shock, where he stayed until he was removed by the police several hours later. Adrian tried several times to speak to Elysia's father. But he was a very stubborn man and thwarted all of Adrian's efforts to find her. Eventually, he put a restraining order against Adrian.

"We were all distraught over the sudden disappearance of Elysia. Adrian spent the next two months in a daze, barely passing his classes. He managed to graduate, then put all his efforts toward finding Elysia."

Speechless, Melina and Serena stared at Angela, wide-eyed, waiting for her to continue her story.

The ladies were brought a cup of tea and a croissant sandwich with a side order of fruit. Melina and Serena were so engrossed in the story they didn't realize they hadn't ordered. Unaffected, Angela continued.

"The months passed by without a clue of Elysia's whereabouts. After being thrown in jail several times by Elysia's father, Adrian finally realized the only way he would find Elysia would be to hire a private detective. Adrian, Jack and I all pulled in extra hours at the equestrian center, but the money was coming in too slowly. So Adrian took a job at the local pub. We were well known among the locals, so he was able to earn quite a bit of money in tips working there at night and on weekends. Finally, after almost a year, we were able to pool our money and hire a private detective. Two long, aching years passed from the time Elysia disappeared until Adrian finally found her."

"Where was she?" both ladies asked in unison.

"Her father had originally sent her to live in a home for unwed mothers here in Atlanta. However, two weeks after she delivered her baby, the home made her pack up her belongings and leave. At that time, she was sent to Ohio to live with some relatives. "

"Why didn't she go back to Scotland?" Melina wanted to know.

"Her father wouldn't let her. He blamed Adrian for ruining Elysia's life as well as her future as an equestrian rider."

"Did Elysia keep the baby?" Serena asked.

"No, she wasn't allowed to. Once she delivered her baby, the nurses took him away before she ever even saw him."

"Him?" Serena questioned.

"Yes, him. The rules were very strict at the home. As soon as the baby was born, it was whisked away to another room. The birth mother was left lying in agony, desperately aching for the loss that she knew would leave an empty space in her heart for the rest of her life. The nurses weren't even allowed to share any information regarding a baby with their birth mother."

"How did she know it was a boy then?" Serena wondered.

"There was a live-in housekeeper at the home, named Anna Marie, who did all the cooking and cleaning. She had a soft spot for these young, yearning mothers. While the nurses treated these women like lepers, never speaking a kind word to any of them, this woman would whisper loving things to them – sharing bible verses with them and softly singing hymns in their ears. The nurses taught the women the wrath of God for their sins. But Anna Marie taught them that we are all sinners and Jesus forgives all of us for our sins. She showered them with the love of Jesus Christ. She also shared with each girl any scrap of information she could gather regarding her newborn baby."

"Thank God there was someone there who was loving towards those poor girls." Serena said.

"Did Adrian come to the states once he realized she was here?" Melina asked.

"Yes, of course. He would have gone to the ends of the earth to find Elysia," Angela exclaimed.

"What did she do when she finally saw Adrian after all that time?" Serena and Melina were both enthralled with Angela's story. Not wanting to miss out on a single detail, they hardly touched their food. The waitress never rushed them, even though there was still a line of people at the door waiting for a table.

"Well, at first Elysia was shocked. She was waitressing at a local coffee shop. Once Adrian arrived in Ohio he went straight to the coffee shop where Elysia worked. Walking in casually, he sat on a stool at the bar. Elysia poured him coffee and asked for his order, never even looking up."

"What did he do?" Melina asked.

"He just sat there looking at her, taking in every detail he had missed over the last two years. Her gorgeous long black hair had been cut very short – almost as short as a boy's hair. She was still just as beautiful as ever, but now had a sadness about her. Dull and listless, her eyes no longer sparkled. When Adrian didn't give her his order, she finally looked up and realized who was sitting in front of her."

"Oh my gosh, she must have been deliriously happy!" Serena exclaimed.

"Actually, no. Not at all. At first, she was very angry with Adrian. She gave him an angry expression and asked him harshly, 'What are you doing here?'"

"That's awful! He must have been devastated." Melina couldn't imagine a worse response.

"Oh, he was. He told her he loved her and how much he had missed her. Elysia looked at him coldly and said, 'Go back home!' She continued working, taking care of all her other customers, never looking back to where Adrian was sitting.

"He loved Elysia and he knew that in spite of all they had been through over the last two years, she still loved him too. He was determined to win back her heart."

"What did he do next?" Melina wondered.

"He went to the coffee shop and sat on the exact same stool at the bar every single day. He never said anything to Elysia. But each time before he left, he wrote a little note on a napkin, saying things like, 'I still love you', 'I'm here for you whenever you are ready', or 'I miss you like crazy.' Each day it was something different. But each time he only wrote one simple line."

"Wow - how long did he keep that up?" asked Serena.

"It took Elysia almost a month before she finally agreed

to talk to him. After the first couple of weeks, he could tell she was starting to look forward to his visits. Her face started to soften when she saw him and her eyes seemed to be getting a little of their sparkle back.

"Not wanting to impose himself on her, Adrian always arrived after Elysia's shift started and left before it ended. He knew in his heart they were meant to be together, so he was willing to wait patiently until she was ready to talk to him.

"One day, when she brought him coffee, she wrote a note on a napkin that said, 'Please stay.'"

The waitress at The Tea Room came to remove their plates. "May I get anything else for you?" she asked.

"No thank you, doll. I think we are finished here. In fact, I think it's time we freed up your table for other customers. We'll be out of your way in just a couple minutes. You have a wonderful Christmas, dear."

"And you have the best Christmas ever." the waitress responded cheerily.

"Thank you, love. You know I will," Angela said sincerely to the waitress.

"You ready, ladies?" Angela gathered her purse and coat and stood up. She gingerly placed her napkin on the table, and headed for the entrance of the restaurant.

Bewildered, Melina and Serena gave each other an odd look. Angela appeared to be indifferent to the fact that their check hadn't yet arrived. Melina stood next to the table watching Serena as she hurried over to catch the waitress before she walked into the kitchen. "Excuse me, Miss? May I get our bill?"

The waitress looked at Melina, then back to Serena. She tilted her head slightly and smiled, "No, love." With those two words, she turned on her heal and headed for the kitchen. She glanced back one more time to Serena and Melina. "Merry Christmas," she mouthed with a nod as she disappeared into the kitchen.

Serena walked over to Melina. They looked at each other in wonderment.

"Where did Angela go?" Serena asked.

Melina pointed to the front door, only to realize that Angela was gone.

Walking out of The Tea Room, the two ladies looked all around for the petite woman. She was nowhere in sight. It was as if she had simply vanished.

Melina and Serena paced back and forth on the sidewalk for a few minutes before finally crossing the street to the parking lot where they originally met Angela.

"Where could she have gone?" Serena asked Melina.

"This is so weird. I will be very upset if she just left, without even saying goodbye." Melina continued looking around, hoping she would appear as magically as she had disappeared.

"Because you want to buy the angel from her?"

"No – because I want to hear the rest of the story!"

Chapter
T E N

As Pappy and Skyler Dawn wandered through the upper level of the mall, Pappy's eyes filled with tears. He now realized that although Skyler Dawn might not understand the exact details of what happened in Bethlehem on that first Christmas morning, she certainly understood what Christmas was all about. In fact, Skyler Dawn just might have a better understanding than anyone.

Pappy looked towards heaven, saying a small prayer to himself, "Thank you, thank you, thank you, my precious sweet Jesus. Now, if you don't mind, I have just one more request. Please help my Anna find her way back to You." Pappy's thoughts were interrupted by a slight squeeze to his hand.

A tiny little voice spoke up, "Pappy, I'm ready to leave now."

"But Cutie, you haven't gotten a present for your mama yet."

"That's okay, Pappy. I already spent all my money."

"Baby Girl, I have some money you can borrow."

Skyler Dawn walked Pappy over to the bench where they both sat down. She looked lovingly at her grandfather. "No thank you, Pappy. My mama doesn't need me to buy her a present for Christmas. All she really wants is for me to draw her a beautiful picture. She doesn't need anything more than that. I spent all my money exactly where I needed to spend it. Mommy'll understand that."

Just when Pappy thought that he couldn't possibly be more proud of Skyler Dawn, she awed him again with her wonderful, innocent wisdom. Pappy held Skyler Dawn's hands in his. "You are so right. How did you get so smart?"

Putting her hands up to Pappy's face, Skyler Dawn kissed him on the end of his nose, then shrugged her shoulders. She took his hand in hers and stood up. "Let's go home now. I have a picture to draw and present to wrap."

"All right then, Cutie. Let's go." Pappy tried to keep up with Skyler Dawn as she skipped towards the car, never letting go of his hand.

Chapter
ELEVEN

In the heart of Buckhead, Anna parked her car in a parking garage on Peachtree Road a couple of blocks from Piedmont Hospital. Finding a parking space near the hospital always proved to be a challenge. No matter what the time of day, Piedmont's parking garage rarely had any spots available. Today was no different. Anna did not find a space until the third lot she attempted. Shocked that she had gone to all this trouble for a stranger, she nervously headed toward the hospital.

Anna took a deep breath, "God, I'm pretty sure you want me to be here. This isn't exactly the kind of sign I was looking for, but I'm going to meet this person anyway. Lord, I know you have lead me here. As hard as this is for me, I'm going to trust that you are going to help me figure out why."

The woman at the information desk stopped Anna. "May I help you Ma'am?"

"Yes, I'm here to see the gentleman who was found on the Marta bench yesterday."

"Are you family?"

"No."

"Do you have any information on who this gentleman might be?"

"I don't know yet. Maybe. I just need to see him."

"Wait just a moment please." The woman walked into the back office and spoke to the manager on duty. She came back to the desk where Anna was waiting. "Normally ma'am, we restrict visitation in the critical care unit to family and close friends. Since we have no information on this gentleman, we are going to let you see him, but you will have to be escorted by a security officer."

"That would be terrific. Thank you very much." Walking through the halls with the security guard, Anna couldn't help but wonder what she was going to say when she finally saw this young gentleman who was embedded in her mind. This was crazy. Half of her wanted to turn around and bolt out of the hospital, but the other half knew she needed to discover her purpose in being there.

"Here's the room, Ma'am. I'll just be waiting out here. Let me know if you need anything." The security guard pulled up a chair and sat in the hallway outside the mystery man's hospital room.

"Thank you." Taking in a deep breath, Anna walked through the door.

Chapter
TWELVE

Standing near their car, Serena and Melina looked for any sign of Angela's whereabouts.

"Here I am ladies." Angela's voice came from behind them.

Serena and Melina jumped. "There you are! We were wondering what happened to you."

"When I saw you turn to go see the waitress, I figured I might as well use my time wisely and visit the ladies room. I had to take care of a few things,"

Both girls gave an embarrassed laugh. "It never even occurred to us to check in there," Melina said sheepishly.

"Well, here we are again. I have much more to tell you. My story has only just begun." Angela sensed that, like herself, Melina and Serena intuitively knew that their meeting was not sheer coincidence.

Dramatically holding her hand across her forehead, Serena passionately proclaimed, "We can't survive without knowing the fate of Adrian and Elysia. Pray tell, do share!"

Smirking at her sister's antics, Melina rolled her eyes.

"What happened the night Elysia asked Adrian to stay? Did she tell him about the baby?"

"Why don't we go for a walk? Let's see, where was I?" Angela looked upward as though she were traveling back to that time many years before.

"Elysia had just asked Adrian to stay," Serena offered.

"Oh yes. That's right. After Elysia's shift ended, she asked Adrian to go for a walk with her. She told him how hurt she was that he never came to the states to bring her back to Scotland. Her father had told her that Adrian knew where Elysia was and if he loved her, he would have come to get her. So, not only did Elysia lose the baby she loved, but she also had spent the previous two years believing that the man she loved had abandoned her."

"That is so sad. I can't believe she thought that Adrian would actually do that to her. It's clear how much he loved her – and so obvious that her father was trying to sabotage their relationship." Melina thought about Skyler. She could never have believed something so ludicrous about the man whom she knew loved her with every inch of his being.

"Yes. That's easy for us to see." Angela offered sympathetically. "But imagine the physical and emotional trauma she had endured over the previous two years. She must have been so hurt and confused from her whole ordeal, she probably didn't know what to believe anymore.

Plus, she had practically placed herself in emotional solitary confinement, not allowing anyone to get close to her. That alone is enough to drastically alter a person's judgment."

"That's true." Melina couldn't imagine the anguish Elysia had endured. "I just feel so remorseful for Adrian."

Angela continued, "By the time she finally told Adrian he could stay, her heart had softened and she was prepared to listen to whatever he had to tell her. He shared with her what life had been like for those two long years - about all the extra hours we worked, the extra job he took and the private detective he was finally able to hire."

"Did he tell her about her father filing a restraining order against him?" Serena wondered.

"Not that night. Adrian knew that Elysia was very fragile after all she had been through. He didn't want to create any more pain for her than she had already endured."

"Wow, I'm impressed. I don't think I would have been so kind." Serena said with awe.

"You would have to know Adrian. He's such a tender man. Even after her father treated him so badly, Adrian still prayed for him."

"Did he ever accept Adrian?" Melina asked.

"Sadly, no. That is a decision I'm afraid he will regret for the rest of his life." Angela looked wistful.

Serena was anxious to hear the rest of the story. "What did Elysia say when Adrian told her he had been looking for her that whole time?"

"She didn't say anything. She simply let Adrian wrap her up in his arms, while she wept all the tears she had been hoarding over the last two years. She wept for their lost time. She wept for not believing in him. But mostly, she wept for the baby she so desperately wanted but had been cruelly taken from her." Tears fell down Angela's cheeks as she thought of Elysia's pain.

Melina got the tissues out of her purse and handed one to each of them. "Did Adrian know the baby had been given up for adoption?"

"He thought that was probably what had happened, but he didn't know for sure until that moment. They both held each other while two years worth of tears spilled from their swollen eyes. Hearing what Elysia had suffered hurt Adrian to the depths of his soul. After they were spent of all emotion and energy, Elysia shared with him that she had delivered a precious baby boy. She told him, 'Adrian, I was so hurt that you no longer cared for me, but as hard as this may be to understand, that didn't even compare to the pain of having my baby ripped out of my arms before he was ever allowed to be cradled in them. I have prayed desperately for

God to heal the empty black hole that consumes my heart. I finally felt God was telling me to name our son. I named him 'Will'. I named him that so God's 'Will' would be done in his life. God gave him to me to carry under my heart for nine months. Finally, I had to give him back to God and entrust Him to take care of our precious son, wherever he may be.'"

By now, Melina, Serena and Angela had settled into one of the benches surrounding the park. The intensity of the story left the two sisters paralyzed with love and sadness for this couple they had never met.

Serena finally broke the silence. "That is incredible. She must be an amazing woman."

"Oh yes," Angela stared into the distance as she went back to that time and place so many years ago. "Adrian brought her back to Scotland to come live with us. She tried desperately to renew her relationship with her father but he refused to allow her into his home. He tore his shirt in anguish and told Elysia she was dead to him. Shortly after that, he moved back to Spain. He turned into an angry, bitter old man before the age of 40."

"That is horrible. The more I hear, the more I wonder about Elysia's mom. What happened to her?"

"Sadly, Elysia's mother died during childbirth. Her father had raised her by himself, which I believe explains why it was so hard for him. He was a very controlling man. And when he couldn't control something, he dismissed it from his life."

"Even his daughter?" Serena asked.

"Even his daughter," Angela looked down in sorrow.

Melina was overwhelmed with her blessings. She had been in the same position as Elysia. Although Melina had lost Skyler, she realized how fortunate she was to have Skyler Dawn, as well as both of their families.

"What happened with Adrian and Elysia?" Serena was good at breaking up the moments of silence.

"They married before they came back to England. Nine months later, Elysia delivered a beautiful baby girl. They named her Faith as a reminder of the faith they had in God's will for their son's life."

"I am so touched by their story. I love the names they chose for their children – especially the meaning behind the names."

"Yes, they are beautiful. Let's keep walking, and I'll finish my story."

Chapter
THIRTEEN

Lying in the hospital bed, the nameless young gentleman looked as though he hadn't eaten in two weeks. Even with his black tousled hair and unkempt beard and moustache, he was obviously a very handsome young man.

"Good morning," Anna sputtered, realizing the young man was awake.

"Good morning." The man looked at her, examining her carefully. "Do I know you?"

Feeling strangely comfortable with him, Anna shared, "I keep hearing a news story about you on the radio. I wanted to see if there was something I could do to help."

Pulling a chair next to his bed, she reached for his hand. He was probably close to the same age Skyler would have been, maybe a little older. Placing her hand in his, Anna felt love stirring deep inside her…a love she hadn't experienced since Skyler died.

"Who are you?" Anna wasn't rude – just curious.

"My name is Billy."

"Do you live in Atlanta?"

"No. My parents are missionaries. We've lived all over

the world, but for the last few years, we've lived in Ecuador."

"What are you doing here?"

"I'm not exactly sure - I felt God calling me here. I tried to ignore Him, but He can be quite persistent," Billy said with a smile. "It took me two years to realize God wasn't going to let me off the hook, so I finally came to Atlanta. If I had been smarter, I would have come during the summer when I could have enjoyed the Summer Olympics," Billy laughed. "Once I arrived, I had no idea what to do next. I had heard that many people travel by the Marta buses or trains, so I thought if I boarded a bus, God would lead me in the right direction."

"It was freezing outside on Saturday. The radio and newspaper said you weren't wearing shoes, socks or a coat. They also said you had no i.d. Were you robbed?"

"Yeah," Billy said. "The big joke in our family is that we are 'protected by poverty' - but my meager belongings were obviously worth something to someone."

"What a wonderful welcome to Atlanta," Anna said sarcastically. "Believe it or not, most people are pretty friendly here – but just like anywhere, we have our share of crime."

"A person passed out on a bus bench is easy prey no matter what town you are in," Billy commented.

"I didn't realize you were unconscious. What happened?"

"I am diabetic. I have had diabetes since I was a toddler. Managing my disease is as normal to me as eating three meals a day is for you. I know what and when I need to eat, as well as how much. By monitoring my activities and judging how I feel, I know when to check my blood sugar. For instance, when I work out my body uses more insulin than usual, so I need to check it more frequently."

"It sounds like you have it under control. But that doesn't explain why you passed out."

Billy looked a little embarrassed. "Although I know how to manage my diabetes in everyday life, sometimes circumstances occur that remind me what a dangerous disease it is. When I was heading for my flight to Atlanta I was running late. I ran all the way from the parking deck to the terminal. I knew if I took the time to check my baggage, I would miss my flight, so I ran all the way through the airport carrying it. By the time I got to the plane, I slumped in my seat, exhausted. It never even crossed my mind to check my blood sugar."

"I don't want to sound like your mother, but you can't be so cavalier about a disease as deadly as diabetes."

"I know. I have already gotten a serious chewing out from the doctor and several of the nurses."

"What happened once you were on the plane?"

"I was feeling run down when we landed in Atlanta, but I still didn't relate it to my diabetes. When I walked through the airport it felt like I was trying to run through a swimming pool. It was like I was trying to move forward but a force was holding me back. I was so relieved when I finally saw a Marta train. I staggered on and fell into a seat. I think at this point I realized what was happening, but I was already too delirious to ask for help."

"Oh, Billy, you are lucky to be alive. Didn't anyone offer to help you?"

"A gentleman helped me off the train and walked me up the stairs, leaving me at the bus stop, lying on a Marta bench. I'm guessing some kids took a look at me, thought I was a drunk and took what they could from me."

"Who finally helped you?"

"I think the kids who stole my stuff are actually the ones who saved my life. I've always worn my medic alert tag on a gold chain around my neck. I believe they thought it was just a necklace when they took it, but quickly noticed it was a medic alert tag."

"What makes you think that?"

"The nurse told me that some kid called an ambulance from the Marta station, giving my exact location. The 911 operator could hear kids in the background yelling, 'C'mon…Let's go, man.'"

"My goodness. It was actually a blessing you were robbed," Anna laughed uncomfortably. "Did they take everything?"

"I didn't come here with much. When you're a missionary's kid, you learn to travel light. I have one thing that I carry with me everywhere I go. It's just a letter that wouldn't mean anything to anybody else, but me. But just in case something ever happened to my wallet, I keep it in a pouch under my shirt. It just attaches to a little elastic belt. I'm really thankful I did that."

"How about your hands and feet? It was below freezing here on Saturday."

"You know, I would love to thank the kid who called 911. He not only saved my life, he also saved me from frostbite."

"It sounds like he is probably a good kid who is involved with the wrong crowd. Who knows, maybe your situation helped him see that. Wouldn't it be great if by saving your life, he ultimately saved his own?"

Billy nodded, saying a quick prayer for the kid who saved his life.

"Do you know when you'll be able to leave here?" Anna asked.

"The doctor said I'll be good to go tomorrow."

"Wonderful! Just in time for Christmas. Do you have anywhere to stay?"

He laughed. "I'll probably just go to an inn, and if there isn't any room, I'll just sleep in the stable. If it was good enough for Jesus, then it's good enough for me."

"Billy, I've really enjoyed talking to you today. I'm glad I met you. Would you do something for me?" Anna asked softly.

"Of course."

"I would be honored if you would join me and my family for Christmas tomorrow."

Anna was shocked at herself. Naturally cautious and practical, she was certainly not the type to invite a complete stranger into her home, especially on Christmas Day.

Billy seemed very humbled by her offer.

Anna walked to his bedside table. "Here is some money for a cab and directions to our home." Anna still couldn't believe what she was saying.

"If the doctors release me tomorrow, it would be my honor to spend Christmas with you and your family."

"Oh, one more thing. What size shoe do you wear?"

"Size 11."

"Terrific! I hope to see you tomorrow. Merry Christmas,

Billy." Anna squeezed his hand then headed toward the door.

"Thank you, Anna, for everything – the visit, the talk and the invitation. Merry Christmas."

Anna felt lighter than she had in years. She went to Lenox Square, the closest mall to Piedmont Hospital, and bought Billy a pair of shoes, a winter coat and a couple of shirts and pants. He was about the same size as Skyler, so buying for him felt perfectly natural. Before going home, Anna dropped off the clothes and shoes at the front desk of the hospital, requesting they be delivered to Billy's room.

For the first time in five years Anna was actually looking forward to Christmas Day. She turned on the radio only to hear the same Beatles song she had heard in the coffee shop. When they sang, *Anna, Go To Him*, it suddenly occurred to her that she had never told Billy her name, yet he called her Anna as she left.

Anna opened her journal and started to write,

Okay God, I'm getting the picture. You really are here. This day didn't turn out the way I expected, but I feel surprisingly peaceful. God, I am so ready to let go of my bitterness. It has taken over my life and stolen every ounce of joy I ever had. Please take this bitterness away from me. I will always miss Skyler...and I'll probably always feel that his death was senseless. I wish you could tell me why he had to die. It's so awful losing a child. But I'm tired of hurting...and I'm weary from being so angry.

With that cleansing prayer, Anna suddenly had a clarity she hadn't experienced since Skyler died. It was as though God was sitting right there, cradling her in His arms saying, *Anna, when my son, Jesus, died on the cross, I was wretched with pain. I watched as they beat and mocked him. I saw them put the crown of thorns on his head. My tears turned to blood when they pushed the sharp thorns deep into his skull. As blood ran down his face, I felt every bit of His pain. I cried in agony as they pounded the long, hard nails through my son's hands and feet. I desperately wanted to save him. It was agony watching my son struggle for each breath. Then when he was thirsty, they gave him vinegar to drink. Crying in anguish, his eyes bore into mine, "My God, My God, why have you forsaken me." Though I wanted to stop his agony, I couldn't - because I loved you and I wanted you to know the joy of living eternally in heaven. When my son died, He gave you eternal life. Don't you get it, Anna? Through Jesus' death, I gave life back. And in Skyler's death, I gave life back. I tried to tell you that but you weren't ready to hear it. Skyler Dawn represents the hope I was giving you for the future. I know your pain, Anna. I know it more than anyone. I've been there too, remember?*

Anna sobbed desperately into her pillow. God knew her pain better than anyone else. God gave her hope four years ago. It was born through a child named Skyler Dawn. What a blessing that child was to all of them. Anna felt peace fill her soul - the same peace she had known before she lost Skyler - the peace that only comes from knowing God. Tearfully, joyfully, she thanked God for his grace and mercy. She knew this was going to be the best Christmas ever.

Chapter
FOURTEEN

Unlike the frenzied shoppers surrounding them, Melina and Serena strolled around the square of Olde Roswell listening intently to Angela's story.

"During the two years Adrian searched for Elysia, he created sculptures from the stones he found lying around the creek that ran behind our house. Scotland has an abundance of a beautiful stone called silver granite. Many of our buildings, spires and columns are made from silver granite. Although covered with mica chips, it is a very durable stone. In the sunshine, silver granite looks as though it has millions of tiny mirrors reflecting the sunlight. Sculpting offered Adrian a release from his stress while giving him plenty of time to commune with God. His faith grew tremendously during those two long years."

"That's incredible. So often people pull away from God during times like that." Melina offered.

"Very true. But Adrian viewed even the most difficult circumstances as an opportunity to grow in his faith. On one particular day he found a silver granite stone that reminded him of an angel. He took that stone and meticulously sculpted it into the most perfect angel I have ever seen."

"The angel you showed us?" asked Serena.

"No, this angel was the first one he ever did. The angel I showed you was modeled after that first one. It was a boy angel with extra small wings, just like the one I showed you. But there was a difference - instead of winking, this angel had both eyes closed in prayer. Adrian believed this perfect angel was God's way of saying, 'If you place your hope and trust in me, you will one day find both Elysia and your baby.'"

"Why did he sculpt a boy angel? He couldn't have known the baby was a boy." Melina questioned.

"No, isn't that neat? Sculpting a boy angel is just what came naturally for him."

"What happened to *that* angel?"

"When Adrian found Elysia, he gave her the angel as a symbol of the faith that sustained him during their separation. Adrian had carved their names into the bottom of the stone. Together they wrote a note to their son Will and took the angel to the home for unwed mothers. They found Anna Marie and asked her to keep the angel in a special place for their boy, just in case he ever came looking for them. Anna Marie took the angel and hugged them tightly. Quickly she shooed them away before they were noticed by one of the sinister nurses."

The three women had come full circle and were again standing in the parking lot. They had only known Angela a few hours, but it seemed so much longer. Angela retrieved the pink jadeite angel from her car and handed it to Melina. "I need to go now, but I want you to give this angel to your daughter."

"I can't possibly take this from you," Melina said.

"Please - I need you to take it. I believe it is the perfect angel for her." Placing her hand over her heart, Angela said with conviction, "I know I'm supposed to give this to you for your daughter. I just wish I could see her face when she opens it."

"You can. Do you have plans for Christmas? We would be honored if you would join us for Christmas tomorrow," Melina encouraged.

"I'm sorry, I can't. But thank you for your kind invitation."

"But we have so many questions about your story," Serena chimed in. "Please, if you have time, at least stop by."

Melina was already writing their information on a piece of paper. "Take our phone number and address. If you have time tomorrow, we would really love for you to meet Skyler Dawn and the rest of our family."

"I will keep your address with me, but don't count on me. Thank you for this wonderful day," Angela said as she was shutting her car door. Serena and Melina stood quietly, wishing for more time with this mysterious woman who had shared so much of herself in such a short time.

Chapter
FIFTEEN

Anxious to wrap Nana Anna's present and draw a picture for her Mama, Skyler Dawn went straight to her house after shopping with Pappy.

"Hey Cutie," Grandma Jenna said when Skyler Dawn walked inside. "It's about time you came home. I've been waiting for you to help me turn this bowl of gingerbread dough into an army of men." She looked at Pappy, "Thanks Curtis. If we don't see you before, we'll be at your house first thing in the morning."

Giving Pappy a huge kiss and hug, Skyler Dawn whispered, "Thank you Pappy. Today was just perfect."

Raising her eyebrows, Grandma Jenna looked at Pappy curiously. With a smug grin he walked out the kitchen door, leaving Grandma Jenna and Skyler Dawn to transform their dough into gingerbread men.

When Curtis pulled into the driveway a few minutes earlier, he had noticed Anna standing by the Christmas tree. Her posture portrayed a confident, content woman...not at all similar to the sad, depressed woman he left earlier that morning. As he entered the house, Curtis thought he heard singing. Not a single note had parted from Anna's lips since Skyler died. It would be a miracle if the music were coming from her.

Too stunned to speak, Curtis stood in the doorway of the living room watching Anna place ornaments on the tree as she sang *Away in a Manger*. Under the Christmas tree lay the nativity scene that had been collecting dust in the attic for the past five years. Amazed, Curtis watched Anna return Skyler's Christmas ornaments to the tree. Overcome with emotion, Curtis walked into Anna's welcoming arms.

"I think it's about time I put Christ back into Christmas," Anna said with a catch in her throat. "And while I was at it, I thought I'd invite Skyler to join us this year, too."

Curtis's eyes were already bloodshot and swollen from the scene at the mall with Skyler Dawn. And now, seeing the change in his beautiful Anna, he wept with thanksgiving for the many miracles Christ had shown him on this perfect Christmas Eve.

Anna picked up the baby Jesus lying in the manger. Handing it to Curtis, she said, "Don't you think we need to wrap the first gift of Christmas?"

Without hesitation, Curtis grabbed the wrapping paper,

tape and scissors. Pausing at the window, he saw a bright, lone star in the barely-lit sky. "Thank you, Jesus!" he whispered.

Chapter
SIXTEEN

Curtis made a huge brunch for everyone each Christmas. It was a tradition they all looked forward to.

"Are we gonna play the alphabet game this year?" Skyler Dawn asked eagerly.

"You bet," Nana Anna replied.

Nana Anna had never participated in the alphabet game before, so Skyler Dawn could barely contain her excitement. She jumped off her chair and ran into Nana Anna's arms.

"Oh, Nana, I'm so happy you're playing with us. Do you want to go first?"

"No, baby girl. Why don't you go first, then I'll go after you."

"Okay," Skyler Dawn looked around the table. "A - I'm thankful for angels. When I see an angel, I feel good all over – even down between my toesies!"

Everyone chuckled at Skyler Dawn's description.

"I'm thankful for angels too," Nana Anna said, squeezing Skyler Dawn in her arms. "I have something this year that

I'm *really* thankful for. I'm not sure if I should share that though. Hmmmm...."

"What, Nana, what? You just *have* to tell us," Skyler Dawn said with her typical impatience.

Nana Anna hadn't played cat and mouse games in years. She decided to tease Skyler Dawn a bit.

"You know what? Why don't ya'll just skip me this year? In fact, let's just skip B altogether."

Skyler Dawn looked at her solemnly. "Nana Anna, you can't just skip a letter of the alphabet. C'mon...tell me! What are you thankful for?"

"Let's see.... what letter was I again?"

"Nanaaaa!"

"Oh yeah, *B*. I'm thankful for...oh, I know, I'm thankful for Billy," Nana Anna said nonchalantly.

Silence filled the room. A quiet murmur followed, eventually graduating into a rumble of curiosity.

The difference in Anna did not go unnoticed by anyone. For the first time in five years her spirit seemed to be alive again. God was definitely working overtime for them this year.

Curtis finally asked the question on everyone's lips, "Who is Billy?"

Anna shared her incredible story from the day before, including all the circumstances that led her to the mystery man in the hospital. After sharing her story, she told them she had invited Billy to spend Christmas with them.

Toward the end of the alphabet, Melina and Serena created another curious stir around the table.

For the letter *S,* Melina said, "I'm thankful for stories. After we open our gifts, Serena and I have a story to share with you all."

It was Serena's turn when they came to *V.* She said, "I'm thankful for visitors. Nana Anna has already shared her visitor with us. Melina and I are hoping and praying that we have a visitor, too."

Not ready to share the details with the family yet, Serena quickly changed the subject. "Okay, Mom, your turn. What are you thankful for that begins with the letter *U?*"

Gramma Jenna spoke up animatedly, "*U* better tell us about your visitor!" "Mommmmmmm!" the twins said in unison.

"That doesn't count. Try again" Melina said.

"Okay, okay, okay. *U* – There is a prevailing optimism surrounding us today. It seems only fitting to say that I'm thankful for 'uplifted spirits'."

"Oh, very nice! I like that one." Curtis exclaimed, smiling at Anna.

As the game ended, Curtis held up his glass in a toast of thanksgiving.

"Here is a toast, to my lovely wife, Anna. Welcome back, honey." A resounding *cheers* was heard with the clinking of glasses.

"May we always be open to the blessings God has available to us," Curtis raised his glass again as a chorus of Amen's sang from the table.

"Now off to the living room we go," Curtis instructed as he stood.

Melina gathered as many plates as she could carry. For the first time in five years, Nana Anna had used her Christmas china – a beautiful pattern Skyler Dawn had never seen.

"I wanna help clean up! I'll be super duper careful!" Skyler Dawn volunteered.

Nana Anna shooed everyone toward the living room. "No, no, no - we are not doing dishes right now!"

Setting the dishes on the end of the table, Melina winked at Serena and Skyler Dawn. All at once, the three of them stood, holding their shoulders at attention. They snapped their wrists towards their forehead in a military salute. All three clicked their heels together, "Yes, Ma'am," they said in harmony, marching into the living room.

Like Curtis, Grampa Alex had been in the military as a young man, so the girls had been doing that in their house for many years. But this was the first time anyone had ever seen all three of them do it in unison.

Joining right in, Nana announced, "Fall in troops! Left, left, left, right, left." She marched them all to the den singing, *Onward Christian Soldiers*. It was so wonderful for all of them to see Nana Anna having fun – especially on Christmas Day. "Don't get too comfortable because I'm going to need each and every one of you. Pappy, do you have the props?"

Curtis went behind the couch to an old cedar chest. He pulled out old potato sacks, robes, scarves, and other garb characteristic of 2000 years ago in Bethlehem.

Smiling at Skyler Dawn, Anna said, "When your daddy was little we acted out the story of the First Christmas, before opening the first gift of Christmas."

"You mean we're gonna open gold, franks, cents and a mirror?" Skyler Dawn asked innocently. Everyone carefully held their laughter so Skyler Dawn wouldn't think they were making fun of her.

"Actually, Cutie those weren't the first gifts of Christmas. But we'll get to that." Pappy distributed the costumes. "Here you go. Skyler Dawn, you get to be Mary," he said, handing her the robe with the light blue hood.

"Who wants to be Joseph?" Curtis asked.

Serena raised her hand in exaggerated excitement, "I do! I do!" Curtis threw Joseph's robe to her.

"We need three wise men. Here you go, Melina, Nana Anna and Gramma Jenna." Curtis threw their costumes to them.

Skyler Dawn burst out in giggles. "Those aren't wise men, silly goose. Those are wise girls!"

In a very deep voice, Gramma Jenna said, "Not today, little girl. Today, we are officially being transformed into wise men. Don't we look smart?" They all three furrowed their eyebrows, trying to look as masculine as possible, while Skyler Dawn crinkled her nose and giggled.

Curtis threw a sackcloth to Grampa Alex.

After checking out the costume, Grampa Alex held it towards Curtis, asking curiously, "What's this one?"

"Check it out again. You'll be able to figure out what it is after a thorough investigation."

Everyone burst out in laughter when Grandpa Alex found the tail of the sackcloth. "Somebody needs to be the donkey!" Curtis laughed.

"What about you, Pappy? Who are you gonna be?" Skyler Dawn asked.

"I, sweet child, am the narrator. Okay, Miss Skyler Dawn, do you know who starts?"

Skyler Dawn looked at her other grandpa. "Of course I

know, silly goose. C'mon, Grampa Alex. I get to ride all the way to Bethlehem on your back. Auntie Serena, I mean, Joseph, you get to walk us there." Grampa Alex galloped toward Auntie Serena with Skyler Dawn on his back. "This is fun! We need to do this every year. Giddy up horsie!"

"Joseph led Mary to Bethlehem on a donkey," Curtis narrated. "They went to the inn where the travelers stayed. Joseph knocked on the door to inquire about a room."

Just then there was a knock at the front door. They couldn't wait to see if it was the man Nana Anna had visited in the hospital or the woman Melina and Serena had mysteriously mentioned earlier. Nana Anna raced Skyler Dawn to the door.

"BILLY!" Nana Anna greeted the young man as though he were a long lost relative. "I'm so glad you are here. You look like you are feeling much better today."

"Yes. I am, thank you," Billy said.

"Please come in and meet my family."

Skyler Dawn reached up, grabbing Billy's hand, as if she had known him her whole life. "Hi. I'm Skyler Dawn - But you can call me Mary."

Billy looked at her quizzically.

"Your timing is perfect," Anna offered. We are reenacting the first Christmas. Guess who's playing the part of Mary?"

Billy looked at Skyler Dawn. "Well hi, Mary. My name is Billy. May I join your play?"

Shaking Billy's hand, Curtis said, "Merry Christmas, Billy. I'm Curtis – Anna's better half."

"That's what he thinks." Anna said laughing.

Holding Billy's hand, Skyler Dawn introduced him to everyone.

"We're glad you could join us. Alex and Jenna live next door with their daughters, Serena and Melina, and our granddaughter, Skyler Dawn," Curtis said, referring to both sets of grandparents. I hope you paid attention because there's gonna be a pop quiz later."

"I'll be ready sir," Billy said with a half smile and nod of his head. "I really appreciate you welcoming me into your home on Christmas."

Pappy shook Billy's hand, "It's a good thing you came. Joseph and Mary just arrived in Bethlehem and we don't have an innkeeper."

Skyler Dawn piped up, "You can be the grumpy guy who works at the hotel."

"You got it," Billy said. "But can I still be the guy at the hotel if I'm not grumpy?"

Skyler Dawn's shoulders slumped, "I guess – but don't forget that there are NO rooms left at the hotel!"

Tossing a sackcloth to Billy, Curtis returned to his narration, "Let's see. Where were we? Oh yeah, Joseph had just led Mary to Bethlehem on a donkey. She was getting ready to give birth to baby Jesus. Joseph was knocking on the door at the inn."

Serena made a knocking sound on the wall.

"I'm sorry, Miss, there are NO rooms left at the hotel." Billy said in a voice that was a perfect imitation of Skyler Dawn.

"BILLLLLLLYYYYYY," Skyler Dawn whined. "She's not a Miss! She's Joseph!"

Billy felt completely at ease with this family. It was obvious the feeling was mutual. "Oh yeah, I'm sorry. Joseph, go ahead and knock again, and I'll do it right this time"

Serena knocked on the wall again then walked toward Billy.

Billy pretended to open a door. "May I help you, sir?"

Serena answered in the most masculine voice she could muster. "Uh yes, please. My wife over here is about to have a baby." Serena burst out laughing. "I can't do this! I just can't say, *my wife*. Here, Billy, switch with me," Serena said taking off her garb to trade with Billy.

Curtis spoke up, "Okay folks. Let's try to actually get through it this time. Innkeeper, you answer the door."

Billy knocked and Serena pretended to open a door. "Hello, sir. May I help you?"

Billy looked very surreal this time. "Yes, I hope so. My lovely wife over here is about to deliver a baby. We desperately need a room."

"I'm sorry, sir. There are no rooms available. The inn is full."

Billy looked distraught. "Please, sir, isn't there some way you can help us? My wife needs to rest. She'll be having the baby very soon."

Serena had completely fallen into the role of the innkeeper, "I'm sorry, sir. The inn is completely full. I do have a stable, though. There is plenty of hay you can use for a bed. With the animals in there, you will be plenty warm. That is all I have to offer you."

Hanging his head, Billy shuffled over to Skyler Dawn who was still sitting on Grampa Alex's back. "Mary, I'm sorry. There are no rooms available. The innkeeper offered his stable for us to sleep in, though. I was hoping to have something nicer for you, but at least we will be able to stay warm."

Completely entranced by the play, Skyler Dawn said, "That's okay, Joseph. I'd love to sleep with the animals."

Billy walked Skyler Dawn and Grampa Alex to the

Christmas tree. Skyler Dawn got off Grampa Alex's back and lay beneath the Christmas tree, pretending to be asleep while Billy pretended to feed Grampa Alex.

Curtis continued, "Mary slept, while Joseph fed the donkey. Before dawn, baby Jesus was born."

Looking at Skyler Dawn, Nana Anna asked, "Would you like to open the very first gift of Christmas?"

"Yes, yes! Can I open it now?"

"Now is the time. Look between those branches."

Skyler Dawn peered between the branches of the Christmas tree until she found a little gold present. "Is this the one?"

"Yes, Cutie, that's the one."

Skyler Dawn took her time, carefully removing each piece of tape before pulling off the wrapping paper. "IT'S BABY JESUS!"

Curtis sat on the floor next to Skyler Dawn. "That's right, baby girl. Why don't you put baby Jesus in the manger with the rest of the nativity scene?" Pappy asked, "So tell me, Sky, what is the first gift of Christmas?"

"Oh – it's Baby Jesus! But what about the mirror and stuff?"

Pappy smiled down at her, "Let's finish our play – we'll get to that."

Pappy started again with his narrator voice. "After Jesus was born in Bethlehem, three wise men traveled from afar to find the King of the Jews."

It was finally time for Melina, Nana Anna and Gramma Jenna to join the Christmas play.

"Did you hear the news?" Melina asked.

"You mean the news that the King of the Jews was born?" asked Gramma Jenna.

"Yes. See that star?" Nana Anna asked pointing to the star on top of the Christmas tree. "We must follow it. It will take us to the new King."

"We can't visit the King of the Jews without bringing him gifts." Melina offered.

"You are right. We need to bring Him the very best that we have." Gramma Jenna said.

"The best gold, the best oil, and the best perfume," said Nana Anna.

Pappy continued, "So the three men traveled far, following the North Star until they finally reached Jesus, the King of the Jews. When they arrived, they offered Jesus the very best gifts of that time - gold, frankincense and myrrh." He accentuated the enunciation of the three gifts.

Pappy patted his knee, motioning Skyler Dawn to sit on his lap. "Do you see, Cutie? It wasn't gold, franks, cents and a mirror. Gold, of course, has always been very valuable. Frankincense was an oil and myrrh was a perfume. They were mixed together to make a precious and sweet smelling oil."

Skyler Dawn's eyes widened with excitement, "Ohhhhh – so those were the *second* gifts of Christmas? I get it now, Pappy!"

"Yes, darling."

"That was fun" said Skyler Dawn, anxious to finish the play and move on to more important things – opening presents. "Now can't we please open our Christmas presents?"

Everyone laughed. "Oh, to be four again." Pappy nodded his head towards Skyler Dawn, "You bet, Cutie, you bet."

Wrapping her arms around Pappy's neck, Skyler Dawn gave him an Eskimo kiss. "Thank you, Pappy. I love you," she said with genuine affection.

Chapter
SEVENTEEN

Searching under the Christmas tree, Skyler Dawn said, "Mama, I want you to open my present first."

Melina was shocked that Skyler Dawn would even consider letting someone else open the first present. "But, Sky, you always open the first present."

"Mama, you silly goose. I *did* open the first present...remember? I opened the very first gift of Christmas. I opened Baby Jesus. Now it's your turn. Be very careful."

The present was wrapped in red Santa Claus paper with four bows taped on the top. It was shaped like a cylinder and covered with no less than 25 pieces of tape. "I'll be super careful, Baby Girl. I promise. Hmm...I wonder what it could be?"

Melina removed the tape and wrapping paper, "A paper towel roll. Just what I always wanted!"

"Mama, you have to look inside the roll, silly."

"Ohhhhh. Okay." Melina said with exaggerated sarcasm. Carefully, she pulled out a piece of paper and unrolled it. As she examined the paper, all color drained from Melina's face. Skyler Dawn had drawn an exact replica of the image in Melina's dream. There was the lavender canopy bed in the middle of the room with Skyler Dawn sleeping peacefully on her pillow. Kneeling next to the bed was a man with Skyler's wavy blonde hair and pale blue eyes. Above his head she had written, "GD NT SNJN." Melina was so choked up she couldn't get out the words she wanted to say. She wrapped her arms around Skyler Dawn's waist and drew her close. Crying in her hair, Melina whispered, "Thank you, Sky. It is beautiful. This is the best Christmas present ever."

Skyler Dawn beamed. She looked at her Pappy and said, "I told you all she wanted for Christmas was a picture."

"I guess you did tell me, now didn't you? What is the picture of, Cutie?"

Skyler Dawn held up the picture so everyone could see it. "This is me sleeping in my bed. And this is my Daddy. He prays with me then sings to me before I fall asleep."

Pappy's eyes never left Skyler Dawn's, "What does it say at the top?"

"It says, 'Goodnight Sunshine', cuz that's what my daddy always says before I fall asleep."

Realizing this picture was the same image as Melina's dream, Serena's jaw practically hit the floor when she saw it.

Billy was quite impressed by the talent of such a small child, but it was clear the picture represented far more than a child's artistic ability.

Anna sat next to Billy, putting his hand in hers. With tears running down her cheeks, she said, "Billy, Skyler Dawn's father was killed almost five years ago. He was also our son. For the longest time I believed God had abandoned me. But now I realize that He has been with me this whole time, waiting patiently for me to allow Him to take away my pain." Curtis placed his hand tenderly on Anna's shoulder knowing how hard this was for her.

"Although most of us can't see or hear Skyler, it sure seems obvious that he is still here. I now realize that God gave us hope through Skyler Dawn." Anna put her fingers to her lips and pointed them in Skyler Dawn's direction as if handing her a kiss. Even with Anna's bright, red nose, puffy eyes, and blotchy face, Pappy thought she never looked more beautiful. Wrapping Skyler Dawn in a huge hug, Anna whispered, "I love you, precious."

Skyler Dawn allowed herself to be swallowed in Nana Anna's arms. Suddenly the child pulled away, pointing her finger at her Nana. Looking very serious she said, "You wait right here. I want you to open my present for you next. I picked it out special - just for you."

Nana Anna started laughing between her sniffles. "Oh no. Someone might as well just bring me the whole box of tissues. I'm not sure I'm going to be able to get through this day."

"I just know that you are gonna love this!" Skyler Dawn said as she gave the gift to Nana Anna.

"I'm sure I will." Anna said, carefully removing the abundance of tape and wrapping paper.

Anna caught her breath when she saw the exquisite angel inside the box. She put her hand to her face, unable to even say thank you.

"I'm sorry, Nana Anna. Please don't cry. I was trying to make you happy." Skyler Dawn said, devastated.

Shaking her head and wiping her tears, Nana Anna managed to whisper, "You didn't make me sad, baby. These are happy tears. This is the most precious Christmas present anyone has ever given me."

"It looks like my daddy, doesn't it?"

"Yes, darling. It looks exactly like your daddy. I can't tell you how much I love it. Thank you."

"It's a music box too, Nana, but they said that part is broken."

"Don't worry about that, baby. It's perfect just the way it is."

"I just knew it was the perfect present for you!"

Looking at Billy with her red nose and blotchy face, Anna laughed through her tears, "You must think we're nuts, Billy."

"Oh, no. My family is very emotional. I feel right at home."

"Well, I'm glad to hear that, because I was starting to think we're all crazy, and I'm the craziest one of all!"

"I really do appreciate your welcoming me into your crazy family." Billy said looking at the music box. "Do you mind if I take a look at that? When my parents were missionaries in Honduras, I was known as 'the kid with the screwdriver.' I used to carry a tiny jeweler's screwdriver with me everywhere I went. Churches would send boxes of American products for the people of Honduras. The problem was, once the products broke, no one knew how to fix them. So I started tinkering with my little jeweler's screwdriver and became pretty good at repairing things. I've worked on plenty of music boxes in my days. May I take a look at this one?"

Skyler Dawn chimed right in. "I told the man that all it needed was the right person to fix it. I bet you're the right person, Billy."

"Well I'll try. Does anyone have a tiny jeweler's screwdriver?" Billy asked.

"Actually, I do." Gramma Jenna retrieved her purse.

"I just knew this thing would come in handy one day." Gramma Jenna said, handing the screwdriver to Billy.

*C*hapter
Eighteen

Melina and Serena were astounded that the angel Skyler Dawn gave to Nana Anna was a carbon copy of the one Angela had given them. It had to be one of the three angels made by Adrian.

"Where did you get that, honey?" Melina asked Skyler Dawn.

"I got it at the mall with Pappy."

"Were there others like it?" Serena asked.

"Nope, it was the only one. I bought it off a cart. The man who sold it didn't want it anymore because it was broken. But I let him know just how 'portant it was and that it's perfect just the way it is."

"I agree with you a hundred percent. Sky, I want you to go next. Open your present from your daddy," Melina said to her daughter.

"Oh, can I? Even though it isn't my turn yet?"

Grampa Alex whined in jest. "Hey, I haven't opened a single gift yet, and this will make two for her."

Skyler Dawn looked at him, wondering if he was serious.

"I'm teasing, you silly goose. I think we all want to see your present from your daddy," Curtis said.

"Grammppaa!" Skyler Dawn said, shaking a finger at her grandfather in chastisement.

Serena retrieved the beautiful pink package sitting all by itself behind the tree. "You are gonna love this, Cutie."

"It's almost as if your daddy picked it out himself." Melina's eyes filled with tears.

Skyler Dawn's eyes grew real wide with anticipation. "Really?" she asked in awe.

Melina nodded. If she spoke, tears would come tumbling out. She could not believe Skyler Dawn had found one of the other angels sculpted by Adrian. She knew that God was doing something special for them on this Christmas day.

Just as Skyler Dawn pulled the bow off of the package, the doorbell rang. Serena jumped up. "WAIT! Don't open it yet."

Holding up a finger to Skyler Dawn, Melina followed her sister to answer the front door.

All eyes were locked on the front door – except for Billy's. Sitting next to a bright lamp, he concentrated on the music box.

Melina and Serena brought Angela into the living room. "God's timing couldn't possibly be any better today. Skyler

Dawn was just about to open the present from her daddy."

"Everyone, this is a very precious woman we met yesterday while shopping for Skyler Dawn's present from her daddy." Melina continued, looking straight at Skyler Dawn, "In fact, I got your present from her."

Serena made the introductions. "This is Angela Saunders."

Skyler Dawn stood; crossing one foot behind the other, she leaned forward to show off the curtsy she had just learned in ballet class. "Nice to meet you, Miss Angela. I'm Skyler Dawn."

"It's very nice to meet you, Skyler Dawn."

"Please meet Skyler Dawn's paternal grandparents, Curtis and Anna. This is their home."

"Thank you for having me here to celebrate Christmas with you. You have a beautiful home."

"We're so glad you are here," Anna said, her face still crimson from crying.

Serena introduced Angela to Alex and Jenna, then finally to Billy, who looked up just long enough to say hello.

Once all the introductions were made, Skyler Dawn looked at her mother pleadingly. "Can I please open my present now?" Skyler Dawn interrupted.

"Yes, precious, you may," Melina winked at her daughter.

Skyler Dawn pulled the pink polka dot tissue paper from the pink bag. Whatever was in the box was very heavy. Skyler Dawn handled it very carefully. Unwrapping the tissue paper, she pulled out the beautiful pink jadeite angel with the extra tiny wings resting at the top of his back.

An overwhelming gasp filled the room. Skyler Dawn was holding the exact replica of the angel she had just given to Nana Anna. "Except for the fact that this angel isn't crystal, it looks exactly like the angel you gave to Nana Anna," Grampa Alex surmised.

Angela did not know about the angel Skyler Dawn had already given to Nana Anna. "That can't be," Angela said. "My son sculpted this angel. He only made three of them. Skyler Dawn couldn't possibly have bought one of the angels. See the initials on the bottom of this angel? Adrian inscribed 'AEWF' on two of the angels and 'Adrian + Elysia' on the third one.

Billy walked slowly toward Skyler Dawn, carrying the crystal angel he had been working on. Everyone in the room watched as he knelt in front of her, holding the two angels next to each other.

Angela was speechless. She slowly moved next to Billy

and Skyler Dawn and gently placed her hands over both angels. She took hold of the angel that Billy had been working on and slowly turned it upside down. Angela felt faint when she saw the initials on the bottom of the angel. Billy helped her into a chair. Once Angela was able to focus, she rubbed her hands over the bottom of the angel whispering the names, "Adrian, Elysia, Will, Faith."

After a few moments, Angela finally spoke. "If I didn't believe in God and know of His miracles, I would say this is impossible." She looked around at the faces filled with curious awe. "I shared much of my story with Melina and Serena yesterday. I would like to share it with you now, if you don't mind."

Chapter
NINETEEN

Angela's story stirred everyone's curiosity "This angel is sculpted from crystal. Skyler Dawn's pink angel, is sculpted from a stone called pink jadeite. There are two very distinct differences between these two angels and the other angel. These angels are actually the second and third ones that Adrian sculpted. The first angel was sculpted from silver granite and had both eyes closed as if in prayer."

Everyone listened as Angela recounted the story of Adrian, Elysia, Will, and Faith. When Melina and Serena thought Angela was finished, she continued, "The part I didn't share yesterday will surely explain why it is a miracle that both angels are here today.

"In January of 1982, Jack and I took Adrian, Elysia and Faith on a two-week holiday to the United States. We spent our first week with dear friends who had moved to Washington D.C. three years before.

"Jack and I planned to remain in D.C. the second week while the others flew to Miami. Adrian was to make an appearance at an Art Show in Fort Lauderdale.

"While Jack drove everyone to the airport, my girlfriend and I took a cab to the retirement home where her mother lived. Do you remember the Air Florida plane crash of 1982 that landed in the Potomac River?"

"Yes, I remember." Anna looked at Curtis, "Remember honey, it was when we were moving from Terre Haute to Dunwoody. We were packing up the den for our move when we heard about it. We were riveted to the television set – praying for the hero in the water. We watched as he helped person after person climb on the rescue ladder of the helicopter. I think he saved five people, then when they went back to save him, he had disappeared into the freezing river. That was such a tremendous tragedy."

"Yes, that's the one. I actually heard the crash. Everyone rushed over to the windows of the retirement center where the sound came from. We could see smoke billowing from the Potomac River. Rumors spread that an Air Florida plane had crashed. People rushed to their televisions to see what happened. Reports finally confirmed that flight 90 had crashed – the same flight Adrian, Elysia, and Faith were taking to Florida. I stood there in shock, watching the television with horror as that plane slowly sunk into the icy cold waters. Each time a person was rescued, I prayed that it would be Adrian, Elysia or Faith. It never was. I watched as that plane was swallowed by the Potomac, carrying my precious son, his beautiful wife and my only granddaughter.

"I was in shock, unable to move. I could barely breathe. The nurses at the retirement home helped me to a back room and brought me oxygen to help steady my breathing. Rocking back and forth, I sat with my hands around my knees, sobbing hysterically. My life, as I knew it, ended in that single moment. My friend just held me.

"All I wanted to do was speak to Jack. I called for him over and over between sobs. But I didn't even know how to get in touch with him. I just wanted him to hold me and tell me it was all a bad dream – that they had missed their plane, or the news was wrong – it was a different plane that crashed.

"Around 5:00 p.m. Jack finally arrived at the retirement home. His face was red and swollen. We fell into each others arms. Neither one of us could speak for what seemed like an eternity. I kept yelling at him, telling him it was a lie; that I wouldn't believe it; that this wasn't a funny joke. Holding me as tight as he could, he whispered the words I never wanted to hear - 'They're all gone.'

"At that moment, a part of me died. I truly didn't know if I would be able to go on living. My reality had become my most horrible nightmare.

"The reason I have told you this is because the angel Skyler Dawn just gave to Anna was on that plane. Faith, almost eight years old at the time, took that angel with her everywhere. We tried to get her to leave the angel in Scotland, but she insisted the angel was her *good luck charm*."

Melina was the first to speak. "I'm so sorry. I had no idea Adrian, Elysia and Faith were no longer alive."

"You seem to have so much inner peace. Considering the losses you've suffered, that doesn't seem humanly possible," Serena commented.

"Sweetheart, it isn't humanly possible. It is only by the grace of God that I am standing here today. I had so much anger and bitterness that I spat hatred at God for taking my family."

"Then how did you gain such peace?" Anna wondered.

"Honey, that is a whole 'nother story. God showed me miracle after miracle until I couldn't resist Him any longer."

"Will you share *that* with us?" Serena asked.

"One day I will. But today isn't that day."

"After I lost Adrian and the girls, I was determined to find my adopted grandson, Will. We stayed in the states for nearly a year after the accident searching for Will. The only thing we found out was that he was born here in Atlanta."

"You finally found Will, right?" Serena asked.

"No, but I never gave up looking." Looking at the angel, Angela whispered quietly, "I can't believe you came all the way to Dunwoody, Georgia, from the bottom of the Potomac River."

Carrying the angel over to the corner of the room where Billy was still sitting, Angela asked, "Do you think you can fix it? I would love to hear this beloved angel make music again."

"I'm not sure if I can, Ma'am, but I will certainly do my best."

"Where is Jack?" Curtis asked.

"Jack passed away five years ago. In 1989, there was an accident at the Equicentre. We had a particularly feisty horse named *Wild Child*, that Jack was determined to break. After nearly two years of working with her, she finally let him sit on her back while she walked around the ring. After Wild Child became fairly tame, Jack wanted to show me all that he had taught her. I watched as Jack led Wild Child into the ring. Just as he was ready to show off some of her new tricks, a hawk flew directly in front of the horses face. She went crazy. She bucked furiously. Jack held on as long as he could, but Wild Child finally won. She threw Jack head first into the fence post. Once freed of her rider, Wild Child calmly walked out of the ring and back into her stall."

"Oh my gosh, what happened to Jack?" Serena asked.

"Jack suffered severe brain damage from the blow to his head. He was in a coma for nearly two months. But once he finally came out of his coma, it still took many months of therapy for him to regain the normal functions of everyday life."

"I'm so sorry," Gramma Jenna was sitting next to Angela with her arm around her.

"Was he able to do all the things he could do before the accident?" Anna asked.

"No, he wasn't. But that was okay. He always had a tremendous amount of kindness but he became even more affectionate and loving after his accident. We loved the Equicentre but I knew without Jack, we could no longer train professional athletes. So we turned the Equicentre into a Christian based riding center for the disabled and mentally challenged. Many people would come to us with no hope left. Jack and I would share our testimonies with them and how we found our way back to God after losing all of our loved ones. People learned that hope always lives, even amid the worst circumstances. My Jack died suddenly last year from a heart attack. I miss him terribly! Once he died, I became more determined than ever to find Will."

"I'm so sorry for your horrible losses. I don't know how you've been able to stay so grounded in your faith," Anna said.

"I haven't always been like this, I assure you. But God tracked me down and would not quit pursuing me until I finally acknowledged Him again. Once I acknowledged Him – the healing began."

"Do you still run the camp for the disabled?" Billy asked, looking up from the angel he was working on.

"Yes, but now that it's just me and my field hands, I shut it down for four months every winter."

"My baby sister has Down Syndrome. I would love to bring her there sometime. I have relatives in Scotland I've wanted to visit. It would be a great opportunity for us to go there," Billy said.

"Billy, you and your sister are welcome any time," Angela responded.

"Angela, are you here in Atlanta all by yourself?" Serena asked.

"I mentioned my dear friend in Washington D.C. As little girls, she and I held tea parties and dreamed of life in the states. Her husband passed away several years ago and she moved to Atlanta to join her son and his family. She became very lonely and depressed right after she got here. One day, she woke up and decided to pursue her lifelong dream of opening a tearoom." Angela looked at Serena and Melina, "She owns the tearoom where we had lunch yesterday."

Melina and Serena had an instant epiphany. "Aha. That's why we were seated right away and were never given a check."

Angela laughed, "Oh, yes. I didn't think about that. I suppose that was confusing."

"Actually, that just added to your mysterious aura," Serena said sheepishly.

"Though I came to spend the winter holiday with my friend, I also had a mission. I prayed I would find information on Will."

"Have you found out anything?" Pappy asked.

"Not yet. I did go to the children's home that was once the home for unwed mothers where Elysia delivered Will. I hoped to find records from the 1970's. There was one woman, Elizabeth, who had been there for nearly 30 years. She had changed dramatically over the years. This sweet woman actually took me out to lunch and shared with me her sorrow for the way she had treated the young mothers.

"In the early 90's, Elizabeth witnessed several miracles and accepted Christ into her life as her personal Savior. Since then, her mission has been to help connect the mothers and children who wanted to be reunited. Unfortunately, there were few records, so the best thing Elizabeth could do was continue working there so she would be available to any former patients looking for information."

"What about the angel given to Anna Marie? Was it still there?" Melina asked.

"No. Elizabeth never saw the angel. But she did say that a few years ago a young man had come looking for information on his parents. Since he knew his birthday she was able to find a file on him. The only thing in his file was a letter from his parents, so she gave it to him."

"Do you know if that was Will?" Melina wondered.

"I'm sure it was. Will was born on December 25, 1971. She said he is the only child they ever had that was born on Christmas Day."

"Did she get his name and address?"

"She did, but Nurse Satina walked in right after Will left. She grabbed the piece of paper out of Elizabeth's hand that contained Will's contact information. Elizabeth later found ashes in Nurse Satina's trashcan."

"That's terrible!" Serena spoke what everyone was feeling.

"What will you do next?" Melina asked.

"I'm not sure yet. When I heard he had the letter from Adrian and Elysia, I felt such peace. Now that I know he has information on us, I believe he will get in touch with me when he is ready. Today would be his 25th birthday," Angela said longingly.

"Angela, now that I know the rest of your story, I have to ask - how can you bear to part with this last angel?" Melina asked.

"That doesn't seem to make any sense does it? For years I have mourned my grandson without even an inkling of hope in finding him. Losing the kids, then Jack, made me accept that there are things I can't control and I have to trust God's will for my life – even if that means accepting something completely different than what I want. When I met Elizabeth and learned that Will had been given the note, I had to rededicate Will to God. That night, I prayed, 'God, I've tried to do this on my own, but now I'm ready to put you in charge. If I am meant to find Will, You will have to lead me to him.'

"I was filled with a peace I barely remembered even existed. Since then, I have felt God telling me to stop placing my faith in this angel and direct my trust where it really belongs – in Jesus Christ. Now I know why God was telling me that. If I hadn't trusted Him, I never would have met all of you, to see firsthand, God's faithfulness. I don't know if I ever will find Will, but this day has reminded me that if I am obedient to God, He will bless me more than I ever could have hoped for on my own."

"I'm amazed at the depth of your faith. I'm not sure I have that kind of faith," Grandma Jenna said.

"You do. Everyone does. God gives you the grace. Whether or not you accept it is up to you. I refused it for several years. I thank God for not giving up on me. It's simply a matter of being willing to give up control. Once we do that, we can trust that God is the one in control. Sometimes it takes us falling into the depths of despair before we realize we don't want that kind of power. I have been there several times in my life. And I am here to tell you, it is only by the grace of God that I am not a bitter old woman!"

Chapter
TWENTY

"*Where's* Nana Anna?" Skyler Dawn asked.

At some point during Angela's story, Anna had quietly left the room.

Concerned, Curtis said, "I didn't see her leave. Does anyone know where she went?"

"I'm right here," Nana Anna said rounding the corner. She walked over to Curtis and hooked her arm in his. "Thank you for loving me these past few years. I turned my back on God after Skyler died. My heart was broken, and I was so angry at God for taking him from us - and from his beautiful Melina and Skyler Dawn." Anna opened her arms for Melina and Skyler Dawn to come over to her. "Melina, you have been such an incredible source of inspiration to me. I truly don't know how you were able to go on with your life and raise a child without her father. And Skyler Dawn, you have always amazed me with how close you have been to your daddy, even though he isn't physically here with you." Then looking at her husband, "And you, Curtis, you also endured the death of a son, yet you always remained faithful to God.

"I know you all have prayed for me these last few years, especially at Christmas." Anna said, looking around the room to her family. "Thank you. Thank you for never giving up on me. Thank you for believing that God could change my heart."

Then looking at Billy, Anna said, "God worked a miracle through you yesterday, and you probably didn't even realize it. You called me Anna as I was leaving your hospital room. In that moment I felt God telling me, 'I know you by name, Anna. You are my child. Trust me. I'm here for you.' How did you know what my name was? I never told you."

Billy looked down sheepishly. "I don't want to take away from what you have been experiencing because your experiences are very real. And God is obviously calling you by name. I almost hate to tell you this," Billy hesitated while everyone waited anxiously. "You were wearing a hospital name tag."

The tension that had filled the entire room disappeared amid the laughter.

Anna went over and put her arm around Billy. "That's okay. God knew it was exactly what I needed at the time. Thank you for agreeing to come over here today. I believe you were very instrumental in God's calling me back to him.

"Now," Anna said, walking over to Angela, "I have a very special present to give." The tears burned in her eyes again. She dabbed at them and took a deep breath. "I hope I can get through this."

Curtis walked up to Anna, urging her to sit down. "Are you okay, honey?"

"Oh yes, darling. I'm more okay than I've ever been." With that, she handed Angela a brown cardboard box. "Merry Christmas, Angela. I believe that God arranged your meeting with these two ladies yesterday, so you would be here in our home today - on Jesus' birthday. God led you here so I could give you this."

Confused, Angela lifted the lid to the box, pulling out its contents. As the tissue paper fell away, there rested a little boy angel praying with his eyes closed. It had extra small wings. The silver granite that it was carved from made the angel appear to have tiny mirrors covering it. Angela couldn't speak. She knew what was on the bottom of the angel without even turning it over. Closing her eyes, she studied the angel with her hands and fingers. She could feel the words, *Adrian + Elysia* carved on the bottom of the angel. Bringing the angel to her face, she ran it across the apples of her cheeks, resting it on her lips. She no longer had control of her emotions.

"Anna Marie?" Angela's throat constricted as she tried to say the words, "You are Anna Marie?"

Anna nodded her head yes and walked over to Angela with outstretched arms. "When I was in my early twenties, Curtis was a POW in Vietnam. I kept myself busy by working at the home for unwed mothers. I knew your beautiful Elysia and your precious grandson, Will.

"If there was ever a mother who should have been allowed to keep her baby, it was your Elysia. She loved that baby so much. She spoke of your Adrian often. She knew that Adrian hadn't abandoned her. But experiencing the grief of having the baby she loved and wanted being torn away from her created all kinds of distortions in her mind. When they took Elysia's son away, she sunk into the depths of depression that no one should ever have to experience. I loved her and tried to comfort her as much as I could, but she was sent away only two weeks after Will was born. I never knew where she went or how to get in touch with her.

"When she returned with Adrian and this angel, I promised her I would keep it safe until Will came for it. Shortly after that, the war ended and Curtis came back home. He was in bad shape after being a prisoner of war for 14 months. I could no longer work at the home, and there was no way I could leave the angel with those cruel, bitter nurses. I snuck into the files and slipped the note in his file.

That way, if he ever came looking for Adrian and Elysia, he would know where to find them.

"Every few years, I would go back to the home around Christmas time, bringing gifts to the new mothers and seeking information on Will. I believed that eventually, the home would be run by loving Christian women, and I would be able to get into the records and find out where he was.

"The last time I went was Christmas of 1991. Just a month later, my Skyler was killed. After that, I questioned God and his 'infinite wisdom' and resigned myself to the fact that I would never find Elysia's Will for her."

Anna was ashamed to admit to Angela that she had given up. Not only had she given up on looking for her grandson, but she'd also given up on her faith in God.

Holding each other, the two women cried for several minutes amid a silent room.

Sensing what Anna was feeling, Angela said, "We've all given up at one point or another. The important thing is that we find our way back."

Silence filled the air, until a little sound of music came wafting from the corner of the room where Billy sat.

"THAT'S THE SONG!" both Skyler Dawn and Melina said in unison as they heard John Denver's song, *Sunshine on My Shoulders* playing from the broken crystal music box.

Skyler Dawn looked at her Mama, "You know this song?"

"Yes, Baby. This is the song your Daddy sings to you before you go to sleep, isn't it?"

"Have you ever been there with him?"

"No, Sky. But I had a dream about your Daddy sitting next to your bed singing that song and talking to you about us and about God. It was a very real dream. I've been going nuts trying to figure out the name of the song that your daddy was singing. I didn't know what to think of the dream until you gave me this picture for Christmas." Melina held up the picture Skyler Dawn had drawn for her.

"Then I knew that the dream was God's way of letting me know that your Daddy is still here with us, loving and caring for us. I was always so sad that you would never know him. But now, I know that you will always know him. Daddy may not be here physically, but he's right here," she said, patting her heart. "As long as we keep our eyes on God we'll always be able to find Daddy, won't we?"

Skyler jumped on her mommy's lap. "That's right, Mommy! I couldn't have said it better!" Everyone treasured Skyler Dawn's unquestionable faith. It was just the refreshing anecdote they all needed.

"Thank you baby. I think we all needed that."

With that, Billy walked over to Anna and handed her the angel music box he had just fixed. "I'll trade you." Anna thought Billy wanted to get a good look at the third angel in the trio - the original angel.

Billy held it in his hands running his fingers over every crevasse of the carved angel. He slowly approached Angela, as he reached inside his shirt and handed her a well-worn note with Adrian and Elysia's handwriting on it.

Angela stared at the note, then slowly looked at Billy. Dropping the note on the floor. Angela tenderly placed both hands on either side of Billy's face – taking in every detail with her fingers. She held his face, as one would a very fragile object.

"Will?" she asked, already knowing the answer.

"My adopted father's name is William. I am named after him. They call me Will, but all my friends call me Billy. It is such an honor to know that my birth parents chose the same name for me, especially knowing the reason they chose that name."

Angela tried to speak but couldn't form the words. She just continued to caress his face and hair. Finally she mouthed, "Happy Birthday, child."

Will spoke to her with unquestionable love. "I want you to know I have had a wonderful life. My adoptive parents were missionaries. Actually, they still are. I grew up all over the world helping my parents share the message of Christ's love. My parents have been very supportive of my meeting my birth parents. They have always instilled in me an incredible respect for God's timing. So, although I had the note that told me my parents were from Scotland, I've never felt the timing was right to go and meet them.

"Oh, Billy!" Angela's heart broke as she realized that her grandson had been sitting here the whole time she was telling the story of Adrian, Elysia, and Faith's death. "I'm so sorry that you had to find out like this about your parents and sister!"

Billy put his arm around Angela. Without a trace of sadness in his voice he said, "Don't be sorry. Our life here on earth is but a heartbeat compared to our life in eternity. I'm still gonna meet them. I'm a very patient person. We have all of eternity to spend together. But in the meantime, I sure am glad God led me here today to meet you. I can't wait for you to meet my mom, dad and little sister. They will be here New Years day."

Stepping forward, Pappy asked everyone to hold hands in prayer:

"Dear Heavenly Father, You have brought us through every conceivable emotion today. We can never express our gratitude for the blessings and miracles you have bestowed on us. What an honor it is to have been chosen by you to help fulfill your awesome plan in so many lives. I claim

James 1:2 and 12 for all of us, which says, *Consider it pure joy, my brothers, whenever you face trials of many kinds, because you know that the testing of your faith develops perseverance. Blessed is the man who perseveres under trial because when he has stood the test, he will receive the crown of life that God has promised to those who love him.* Every one of us here has been tested, dear Lord. Your love and amazing grace have seen us through pain and sorrow. Thank you, Sweet Jesus that we have all found our way back into your arms. Thank you for pursuing each and every one of us. In Jesus' name we pray, Amen."

Like the first lone star of the night, *Silent Night* resonated through the room in a single voice, slowly to be joined by all the others.

Psalm 39:5, NIV: *You have made my days a mere handbreadth; the span of my years is as nothing before you. Each man's life is but a breath.*

Order Books Today

The Christmas of Miracles

makes the perfect Christmas present for

family, friends, teachers, bus drivers,

co-workers, delivery people...

just about anyone you can think of.

To place an order, call 770-888-5515

or visit the website at

www.FourSonkistAngels.com

To receive regular updates on

Michelle's future books

and upcoming engagements,

send an email to

info@FourSonkistAngels.com

or check the website at

http://www.MichelleBaileyWebster.com